Valerie Ann Gyurko

Here, Buster!

(Orig. title: SEA PUP)

BY ARCHIE BINNS

Illustrated by Robert Candy

Cover by Bernard Krigstein

SCHOLASTIC BOOK SERVICES

Published by Scholastic Book Services, a division of Scholastic Magazines, Inc., 33 West 42nd Street, New York 36, N.Y.

Other books by Archie Binns
The Enchanted Islands
The Headwaters

2nd printing.........................October, 1961

Printed in the U.S.A.

CONTENTS

1. CLINT BABY-SITS

REMEMBER, Clint, no sailing after dark."
"I'll be back for supper, Mom; maybe earlier." Clint carried his breakfast dishes to the sink, where his mother was whipping up suds in the dishpan.

"And do be careful, Clint." This from Aunt Harriet, who was visiting from Seattle. Aunt Harriet wore glasses with horn rims and she taught school, and she seemed to think you were in danger when you got off a paved street.

1

"I'm always careful, Aunt Harriet."

Clint had his mother's dark eyes, but he was fair like his father and tall for thirteen. He was in junior high, and he did the chores on their small farm before and after school because his father, Jim Barlow, was generally busy with his truck logging. Clint didn't often get a whole day off, and now that he had a precious Saturday he wasn't going to have any of it spoiled by women. He slipped into his leather jacket, and was hurrying out when his mother noticed his empty hands.

"Where's your lunch?"

"I won't need any, Mom. I'm going to live off the water—like a castaway."

"You must take something—just in case."

"O.K. Just emergency rations, though." While he stuffed a few rounds of pilot bread and a piece of smoked salmon into a paper sack, his mother slipped in three oranges.

Aunt Harriet began worrying again. "It doesn't seem right for a boy to be out alone in a sailboat all day—"

Clint left before his aunt could talk his mother into keeping him home.

Women! Mom was all right, but Aunt Harriet was what you'd expect of a woman who went to college in the East while her sister married a Puget Sound logger. She thought Clint should go to Seattle when he was through junior high; it wouldn't be right for him to go to a country high school in this wild place.

If it was wild, he liked it that way. Hood Canal was five miles wide where they lived, divided to the north by the great wooded headland of Toandos Peninsula. From their kitchen window he could see shores and coves he hadn't had a chance to visit.

It was the first time that spring he had earned a whole day for exploring—and a precious half hour had been wasted. Lunch! He looked disgustedly at the bag as he started toward the beach. Today he was going to prove that he could get his food and fresh water from the sea. He was going to try out his plankton drag—the water around there was alive with food. For fresh water he would squeeze the juice of raw fish, or condense his breath by breathing into a bottle. But try to explain to women that food is all around you! And fresh water, too!

The dogs trotted beside him to the beach —Wolf, the half-police dog, and Jerry, the small Airedale.

"No dogs this time," Clint told them as he put a roller under the keel of his sloop

Dolphin. "This is a scientific expedition; you wouldn't like breathing into bottles."

The dogs whined with excitement, then disappointment as he shoved his little sloop off and jumped in, pushing out farther with an oar. Jerry had all four feet in the water and was ready to swim.

"Go back, Jerry!"

It was still fresh morning, with traces of mist on the water and a feeling of newness about the world. But it was too late for Clint to pretend that he was the first Indian setting out on a voyage of discovery. A black power cruiser was trolling off the end of Toandos Peninsula, though it was too early in the year for anything but young salmon, called "jacks." In the opposite direction a heavy skiff was driving up from the south—old Joe Horton's boat; maybe he was coming to visit.

From the direction of the slack cruiser came the sharp crack of a high-powered rifle. Clint listened for another—but if there was a second shot, it was drowned out by Joe's motor. As Clint hesitated, with the main halliard in his hands, the racket of the outboard sank to a sputtering and Joe bellowed:

"Ahoy, Clint! I got something to show

you!" He shut off the motor and Clint caught the gunwale of the skiff as it came alongside. Joe held up a quart jar.

"It's the darnedest thing ever—a jellyfish shaped like a real fish!"

While Joe held the boats together the boy studied the translucent thing swimming in the jar. It was over two inches long with a big, round head and floppy tail like an ornamental goldfish.

"Where'd you find it, Joe?"

"Right beside my float."

"Wonder why it came to the surface?"

"You know what it is?"

"It's a nudibranch," Clint said; "a kind of sea snail without a shell. You don't often see one because they stay near the bottom."

"It beats me." Joe's old eyes lit up with pride. "I been on Puget Sound sixty-five years; I find something I never saw before and you know right off what it is! How long you been around?"

"I'm thirteen."

"It beats me!" Joe repeated.

"Aw, it's just that I've been studying about things in the water—" There was another distant rifle crack. "What do you suppose they're shooting at?"

"A seal, probably," said Joe. "I got a shot at one yesterday. Missed him, though." He looked at the creature in the jar. "You want it, Clint?"

"I'd like to make a drawing of it."

Joe put the jar in Clint's boat. "It's yours."

"Thanks, Joe."

The old man gave his starting rope a pull and his motor roared. "So long, Clint."

"So long!"

Clint hoisted the *Dolphin's* mainsail, then the jib. He settled himself aft and let the sails draw. As he put up the tiller, the sloop heeled over a little and slipped away. In the clear water he could see bullheads dart and stop; a sand dab on the bottom speckled to look like pebbles; and dark seaweed waving in the incoming tide. Then the beach dropped out of sight under deep water.

The first time Clint remembered looking into water was at Pleasant Harbor, near his father's log boom. He was two or three years old then, and his father had him out on one of the floats. The water in the distance was blue, but in the harbor it was like green grass that you couldn't see through. He lay on the float with his face over the edge while his father held on to his overalls' straps, and he found that where he made a shadow he could look deep into the water. There was another world down

6

there, with big fish sailing through the water or eating off barnacle-covered piles. Far down there was green and purple seaweed waving like trees in the wind.

He couldn't remember any more, but afterward he used to see it in his dreams: fish sailing through the dim green underworld and seaweed waving in the tide. When Clint was older, his father told him that all life had come out of the ocean.

That was about the time Mom gave him a little book called *Animals of the Seashore*. He began finding out everything he could about sea life and collecting shells and things. Later he got other books. Old Joe was amazed that he knew so much about the sea; but Clint didn't feel that he knew anything yet—he was just starting to learn.

While the boy had been thinking of other things he had come up to the black power cruiser which was lying to off Oak Head. One sports fisherman was gaffing a jack salmon—a young king—which the other had brought alongside.

Clint hadn't intended to stop, but he wanted to find out about the shooting. He steered for the cruiser and as he sailed in close, someone bellowed:

"Hey, boy, keep off!"

The sails fluttered as the *Dolphin* came up into the wind and moved alongside the other boat without bumping, Clint held onto the cockpit coaming with one hand while he let go the halliards. When the sails were down the little sloop wasn't a menace any more. The big blond fisherman, who had told him to keep off, said:

"You sail all right, boy!"

"How's fishing?"

"Not so good." Fishermen always said that—even when it was good.

"He's kidding!" the other said. "He shot one that weighed three hundred pounds!"

"*Ja*, a seal. I plugged him, all right."

"After six shots," the other fisherman said.

"Five. It was a foxy one," the big man explained to Clint. "Every time I fired, it dived. But it kept going after the fish my partner was playing. The last time I plugged it good."

"Have you got the seal?" Clint asked.

"He sank." The big man pointed downward with his thumb. "Yust the place for the old salmon stealer."

Clint had a look at the fishermen's catch —three jack salmon—and cast off. The one thing he would have liked to examine was the seal—and they hadn't saved it. Why did they have to shoot it, anyway?

The rest 'of the morning he sailed in deep water, towing his plankton drag, and breathing into a Coke bottle with a glass tube through a cork.

Clint had made the plankton drag himself, with a little help from his mother. It was a cone of fine cloth that strained out water while it collected the tiny animals and plants that fill the sea like drifting dust. Smaller things in the sea fed on plankton and diatoms, and the larger things fed on the smaller ones. Anyone with a plankton drag could collect nourishing food from the sea, even if he never saw a fish. That was one of the things Mom and Aunt Harriet couldn't believe.

The Coke bottle with the glass tube was simple, but it was scientific, too. Clint had read about it in an old article by Alexander Graham Bell, the man who invented the telephone. At sea level there is so much moisture in the air that you are breathing out vapor all the time. When you breathe into a bottle the vapor condenses; by doing it all day you get enough water to keep alive. Clint was never going to be cast adrift in a lifeboat without having something of the sort along. It was tiresome, of course, and it took hours to collect a little water in the bottom of the bottle. He wasn't sure he wanted to drink it, anyway.

In the early afternoon Clint pulled in his plankton drag. Sure enough, the bottle in the center had enough solids for a meal. But though he was hungry, the watery dust of tiny animals and plants didn't tempt him. He sampled it, then decided to continue on to Pirate Bay, around the next point of land, and have an oyster roast.

As he came into the bay he raised the centerboard and sailed up on the beach where there were fewer oysters to scrape the bottom of the boat. He took in the sails and went ashore with the anchor.

The bay was a mile wide and its narrow beach ended in drift logs and brush at the foot of high yellow cliffs. A madrona tree with smooth, red-brown bark leaned out from the foot of the cliff near the spot where Clint stood. There wasn't a sign that anyone had ever been there before. It was a place for pirates.

Clint gathered driftwood, and broke twigs from a dead bush for kindling. He had a fire blazing by the time the incoming tide refloated the *Dolphin*. He pulled her farther up the beach and started gathering oysters. There were small ones, medium ones, mature ones a foot long, and oysters that had grown together in clusters he could hardly lift. He selected an armful of smooth, medium ones and carried them to his camping spot.

When the fire burned down, Clint put the oysters in the coals, saving out a few to eat raw after examining them for pearls. He found three in one oyster; they were the size of pinheads. Pearls were supposed to be valuable, but he had never heard of anyone selling any of them. He kept his in an egg cup—some of them as big as BB shot.

Clint knew the big oysters hadn't been on Puget Sound very long. The seed had been brought from Japan and tried out in oyster beds. Every year the tides carried their spawn to new places, and now they were everywhere. It looked as if they might crowd everything else off the beach and upset the balance of nature.

He stopped worrying about the balance of nature when the wonderful smell came from the opening shells on the coals. If there were ever too many oysters they could be taken care of by letting enough people get a whiff of oysters roasting on the beach.

As each oyster reached the right shade of golden brown, Clint lifted it out of its shell with his knife. When he was through, he had twenty-six empty oyster shells beside him. If he had roasted more he would have eaten them, and he was glad he hadn't. Drowsy and full of oysters, he put more wood on the fire and stretched beside it to rest a while. The spring afternoon had a chill in it and the fire felt good.

He was almost asleep when he heard what sounded like the bleating of a lamb—a most unlikely thing because the lamb would have had to swim to get there, or come down the steep cliff. Not even a young goat could have done that—unless an eagle carried it. But eagles don't take young animals down; they take them up—to their nests. . . . Besides, there are no more eagles on Puget Sound.

The bleating came again. He sat up, and it stopped. Maybe it was so far away he could only hear it with his ear to the ground. No—there it came again, from farther along the beach.

Clint was wide awake now. The lamb must have fallen over the cliff, so he would look for it at the upper edge of the beach. He walked along the drift logs, and pushed through alders with new spring leaves; but there was no sign of any lamb. When he was sure he had passed the place the sound had come from, he walked toward the beach to a cluster of boulders. He stood there listening intently when it came again, so close it almost made him jump—a thin bleating somewhere near his feet. He walked around a granite boulder and saw something white move on the sand.

Ma-a-a-a! . . . It was white and woolly, but it wasn't a lamb. It was a baby seal that raised its head and sounded off impatiently. Its bleat was like an angry little horn calling its mother home from the sea.

Ma-a-a-a-a!

"Sound off, Buster!" Clint said. "Your ma'll be here soon."

It was the first baby seal Clint had ever seen—about two feet long, with big brown human-looking eyes, and dark, determined little whiskers, and upstanding eyebrows on its white face. It was a harbor seal—the only kind native to Puget Sound.

Ma-a-a-a-a!

"Keep it up, Buster! She'll be here soon."

The seal quieted at the sound of Clint's voice and began nuzzling his ankle. He wanted to pick it up and hold it in his lap until its mother returned; but he had heard that some animals abandoned their young if they have the scent of human beings on them, and he didn't want that to happen to this husky little fellow.

13

Ma-a-a-a-a-a!

"All right, Buster. I'll baby-sit you till your ma gets back."

Clint sat on a low granite boulder, sheltered from the wind by a larger one, and scanned the choppy water. There was no sleek seal head anywhere in sight, and the wide water looked cold and lonesome. His boat was bumping on the beach again and he went to pull it farther up. The mother seal might not come ashore if she saw him, so he went back to his fire. It had burned down to ashes, but he was afraid to put on more wood because the blaze might scare the mother seal away.

It was cold and it was getting late. Clint wondered why he was waiting. He couldn't do anything for the baby seal, and his being there wouldn't bring the mother until she was ready to come back.

Maybe the mother seal wasn't coming back. Maybe she was the seal the fishermen had killed in the morning.

Ma-a-a-a-a-a!

The baby seal was telling the world that his mother had forgotten him.

Clint scanned the choppy water; there was nothing that looked like a home-coming seal. He walked back to the boulders. The woolly white baby bleated more insistently as he came near. It quieted when he sat on the low rock and talked to it.

"I don't know, Buster," Clint said. "Things don't look so good. I'll wait a while longer for your ma, then I'll have to be going."

The seal had turned and was butting and nuzzling Clint's ankles again, making little coaxing sounds. It seemed to think Clint was its mother.

"That's the way it is, Buster," Clint went on. "People have it in for seals, because they like salmon and they're smart. People shoot seals whenever they get a chance." He remembered that he had shot at seals, and he apologized. "I've shot at them with my twenty-two. I never hit one. I don't know why I did it. That's another thing about people—they don't think."

"You're hungry," Clint said, "but at least you aren't cold." Clint was shivering and he knew that he should be on his way home.

"Well, Buster," he told the little seal, "if your ma isn't back by sunset, I'll have to shove off."

Ma-a-a-a-a-a!

"I know." He patted the woolly little head. If the mother came back after all this time she wouldn't mind the human smell on her baby. Besides, Clint's hands smelled mostly of smoked salmon and oysters.

Clint waited, shivering, until the sun touched one of the high foothills of the Olympics and slipped down behind it.

"I'll give your ma one more chance, Buster."

He stood on a rock, scanning the wide, choppy water that reflected broken bits of the sunset; but there wasn't any sign of a sleek, round head.

"You're an orphan, Buster."

Ma-a-a-a!

Clint looked worriedly at the little white seal nuzzling at his feet. Then he knelt and gathered it into his arms.

"I don't know what the folks will say, Buster, but I can't leave you to starve."

While he was carrying the seal to his boat he seemed to learn more about it than he had by watching it for hours. Its tapering, streamlined body was something you'd expect to be made of cold metal. Instead it was warm and friendly, and wiggly.

The seal wasn't like himself, but it was made for things he wanted to do. It was streamlined and powered to swim far and deep; and it had warm blood and a warm heart to enjoy the experience.

2. BUSTER COMES HOME

IT WAS dark when the *Dolphin* came booming in toward Barlow's Landing. Clint could see the black shape of Kirby Mountain against the sky, and below the notch in its side the lighted windows of his home. On the beach a flashlight blinked, shining on the dark rough water and showing Clint where to land. The warm lights of the house looked good, but when he got there he would have to face some music. He had promised to be home for supper,

17

and supper must have been over an hour ago.

He could hear the friendly barking of the dogs, and the rush of waves on the beach. He pulled up the centerboard and sailed directly for the light.

The keel grated on gravel, and the grating changed to a hollow rumble as his father caught the bow of the boat and hauled it up on the waiting rollers. In a second Clint was out helping him. Neither of them said anything until the boat was above the high-tide mark.

Then his father asked, "Well, Clint?"

Ma-a-a-a-a!

The little tin-horn bleat answered the question and started the dogs barking furiously—and Clint and his father were kept busy holding them back.

With one hand on Wolf's collar, Jim Barlow turned the flashlight into the boat.

"What's this?"

In the beam of the flashlight the little seal looked very white, and its brown eyes blinked as it rasied its head. It had saved Clint from a bawling out.

"It's an orphan, Dad. The fisherman killed its mother. It isn't more than a day old. I couldn't leave it to starve."

"Cute little fellow," his father said. "What are you going to do with him?"

"I've got to take care of him until he can look after himself, Dad—and it's my first chance to study a seal."

His father sighed. "It's going to be a peck of trouble. Bring it along and see what your mother says; it's up to her."

Clint was shivering as he stumbled up the path behind his father, hugging the little seal in his arms; it was the only warm thing in the windy night. In the brightly lit kitchen everything was warm; but Clint was uneasy because his new friend was unwelcome.

"A *seal*, Clint?" his mother objected. "You *can't* keep it!"

"I've heard that they get to be terrible nuisances," Aunt Harriet said. "If you're wise, Clint, you'll put it back in the water right now and save yourself a lot of trouble."

"It's never been in the water, Aunt Harriet. It would drown!"

"Imagine a seal drowning!"

"It has to be taught to swim," Clint explained. "Seals used to be land animals—"

His father came in carrying a box with some feed sacks at the bottom.

19

"Here." He set the box beside the stove. "Put him in here."

Clint was still shivering as he put the little seal in its bed. His mother poured a big cup of coffee from the pot on the stove.

"Sit down and drink this, Clint, while I get you something to eat. You've got a chill, and no wonder, gallivanting around on the water at night with a seal!"

Clint drank the hot coffee and his shivering stopped. Then he washed at the kitchen sink while his mother fixed a plate of roast venison and sweet potatoes.

"Now get some food into you."

He sat down gratefully. The venison tasted good to him after a day of seafood.

Ma-a-a-a-a!

"He's hungry." Clint started to get up. "I'll fix him some milk—"

His mother sat him down again with a firm but friendly push.

"You'll eat first!"

Aunt Harriet was kneeling beside the stove, looking at the seal.

"What an odd little creature. I'll fix him a saucer of milk."

"Make it a bottle," Dad advised. "It's not a kitten."

Clint's mother poured milk into a sauce-

pan. "There's the bottle we got for the calf
—on a shelf in the garage."

Clint started up again. "I'll get it!"

"You finish your supper," his father told
him, going for the bottle himself.

The boy gulped the last of his food before the bottle was washed and filled.

"I'll feed him!"

But Aunt Harriet took the bottle with a
professional air, shaking a few drops from
the nipple onto her wrist.

"It feels all right. What is a seal's body
temperature?"

"The same as ours, I think." Clint didn't
know for sure, but the seal had felt warm
when he carried it. He was jealous of his
aunt's attention to the little fellow; she was
taking over as if she had found him.

"Here, fellow." She held the bottle at
arm's length. "Here's your milk."

In its eagerness the seal pushed the nipple aside and nuzzled her hand. She drew
back out of reach.

Ma-a-a-a-a!

Aunt Harriet started at the angry little
bleat and drew back farther. She tried once
more, gingerly, then handed the bottle to
Clint.

"Here. Let's see what kind of nursemaid
you are!"

21

Clint had the advantage of knowing there was nothing to be afraid of; and the seal pup was used to his voice.

"All right, Buster, here it is."

Time after time the seal made connection with the bottle, only to spit out the nipple and nuzzle for Clint's hand. Finally Clint wet the nipple with milk and the seal took it, doubtfully at first, then eagerly. He drank with little whimpering noises, looking up as if to say he had known all along that Clint was his mother.

Dad and Mom left the kitchen when they saw that Clint was managing, but Aunt Harriet lingered.

When the bottle was half empty, Clint wrested it away.

"You're drinking too fast, Buster. It's not good for you."

"Don't you have to burp him?" Aunt Harriet asked.

Ma-a-a-a-a!

"He says no."

The pup seemed hungrier than ever. Clint fed him the rest of the bottle, then the remaining milk from the saucepan on the stove. After that he talked the little fellow into being quiet; and he washed the bottle at the sink along with his own dishes. He wasn't always so neat when he had had a snack in the kitchen, but he knew the trouble that comes when parents have to look after pets. And this one wasn't even accepted yet.

In the box beside the stove the little seal was nodding, its eyes almost closed. It looked like a Christmas lamb, and Clint thought it the most beautiful thing he had ever seen.

"Good night, Buster." He turned out the light and tiptoed away.

As he came into the living room his elders stopped talking. That was a sign of trouble. He stretched himself in his favorite spot in front of the fireplace; and his father went on with what he had started to say at the beach.

"Well, Clint, you know the rules."

"Yes, Dad."

"You were out sailing two hours after you had promised to be home. You could have capsized, or stove your boat on a drift log in the dark." Jim Barlow's voice was soft and easy, like the comfy slippers he used in the house when he took off his logging shoes with the steel caulks.

"That's right," Clint said.

"You're not to take your boat out for the next two weeks. Don't forget it."

"Fair enough, Dad."

23

"About the seal. You were right—you couldn't leave it to starve. But don't count on keeping it. If I know anything about seals, it'll be a nuisance. You can look after it until we decide what to do with it, or until it makes too much trouble."

"Thanks, Dad. I'll see that it isn't any trouble to you or Mom."

His mother smiled over the wool sock she was darning. "That's a big promise, Clint, but we'll see. Now you ought to go to bed. You were out late and you got chilled."

Clint got up obediently. He had to be on his best behavior to make up for any mistakes of Buster's. He took one more look at the seal. It was safe and warm and full of milk—sleeping like a log.

Upstairs in his room Clint was close to the gusts of wind and rain that swept over the roof, and through their sound he could hear the cold wash of waves on the beach. It was a good night to be indoors, going to bed early; he felt as safe as the little seal in the box by the stove. He didn't feel bad about being forbidden to go on expeditions for a while; it showed that his parents cared for him.

He undressed with Scammon's *Marine Mammals of the Northwest Coast* open on his table among shells and agates and dried sea fans. It had a lot to say about seals. Clint wondered how far he could trust such an old book. But maybe seals hadn't changed much since 1874.

Clint's first thought on waking was of the seal pup. Was it making a fuss and waking people up? He didn't hear anything. He looked out of the window while he dressed. It was gray and wet outside, with a broad streak of light above the distant mainland, and the end of high Toandos Peninsula looked like the bow of a great ship.

He heard the rattle of a stove lid as he went downstairs, and then a faint whimpering. His father was in the kitchen, fully dressed, making a fire in the range.

"Morning, Clint."

"Good morning, Dad."

His father touched a match to pitch shavings in the firebox and the answering blaze lit up his face with a strong yellow light.

"Your friend seems to have got through the night O.K."

Clint went around his father to the other side of the range and stared in wonder. Last night there had been a white seal on brown gunny sacks; now there was a

25

mottled gray-and-white seal on a bed of white!

"Dad, he's changed color!"

"I noticed." His father looked at the seal again. "Shed his baby fur."

Clint touched the lightly matted white stuff beside the wiggling pup.

"He's rolled it into a bed for himself!"

Ma-a-a-a-a!

"Hungry," Dad commented. "At least you didn't have to give him a two o'clock bottle, like your ma used to give you."

"I'll fix him one now." While Clint was getting the milk ready he thought it was a good sign for his father to talk of the time when he was a baby. It showed that he was still friendly toward young things.

Ma-a-a-a-a-a!

"It's coming, Buster!" Clint put the saucepan of milk on the range that was just beginning to warm up.

His father took the milk pail from its shelf.

"I'll do the milking this morning. Funny how cows don't sleep late on Sundays."

Ma-a-a-a-a-a!

"Or seals, either."

"I'll do the rest of the chores when I've given him a bottle, Dad."

"Good. We don't want him to wake up the women."

After his father was gone, Clint squatted by the box, visiting with the little seal. Its new coat had a smooth, oiled feeling and it shone as he stroked it, brushing off stray white hairs.

"There, Buster, that's the last of your baby clothes. You're a big boy now, and your breakfast's getting warm." Clint didn't know how mother seals talked, but Buster seemed at home with his voice. When Clint talked to him the little seal didn't bleat; he only raised his head and made friendly little whimpers.

Clint put more wood in the range and dipped his finger in the milk three times before he decided it was warm enough. While he fixed the bottle, his new friend bobbed his head up and down, begging eagerly.

"Here, Buster, come and get it!" Buster fumbled a moment with the nipple, then fastened onto it and drank contentedly.

"Good boy," Clint said. "You're learning fast; you're growing up already!"

Clint wasn't just flattering. Since last evening Buster had lost his baby wool, had adjusted to his new home and accepted

Clint as his friend, and had learned to connect with his bottle on the first try.

He had to leave Buster while he went to do the morning chores. But thinking of the lively little seal made everything else seem more alive. The night's wind and rain had changed to a light April drizzle, with a promise of sunshine. In the world of new leaves and new grass there was a rainbow feeling in the air. Carrying armfuls of wood from the shed to the box that was filled from the porch, Clint breathed the good smell of split fir and admired the creamy wood and soft brown bark—things he usually didn't take time to notice.

In the chicken yard, too, there was that rainbow feeling when he thought of his new pet. Under the shed roof, Clint scattered wheat for the clucking New Hampshire Reds and tried to think more scientifically about seals.

Millions of years ago their ancestors had come out of the sea and changed to animals that looked like bears. Later the bearlike animals went back to the sea; their legs changed to flippers, and they learned to swim like fish.

No one knew just why they went back; but Clint saw how it could happen. In the fall, bears go to the creeks to fatten up on

salmon. It wasn't hard to imagine some of
them going to the mouth of a creek, where
the salmon were fresher. Some of them
might swim out a little way, after the
salmon. If they kept doing that long
enough . . .

"Clint!"
He started at the sound of his aunt's
voice. She was standing under an umbrella
at the end of the open shed, smiling at him
anxiously. He didn't know how long she had
been there while he stood with the empty
chicken-feed pail in his hands, dreaming of
seals.

"Yes, Aunt Harriet."

"Breakfast is ready."

"I'll be right there."

She waited while he put the feed pail
away. When they were walking to the house
she suddenly asked:

"Clint, do you think you should keep that
seal?"

"Dad and Mom said I could, if I look
after it."

"I don't think you should. You need play-
mates—boys and girls your own age."

"I have friends at school."

"Not just at school. Boys and girls to go
to parties with, and fishing, and boating."

29

Clint was glad when they reached the house. He was also glad Aunt Harriet was going home that afternoon.

"Buster will be good company when he grows up a little. You'll see."

"He belongs to one world, and you belong to another," she told him. "You don't want to get mixed up and sacrifice yourself for the wrong world."

Clint didn't answer. He thought of his aunt as a woman from the East, where people weren't very real and talked a lot to hide it. She was making a big problem out of a simple thing like a pet seal.

He opened the kitchen door, and Buster raised up in his box to whine an eager welcome. As Clint patted the friendly little head the bothersome talk went out of his mind. Words didn't seem to mean much just then.

3. BUSTER LEARNS

CLINT no longer had to fix a morning bottle. Buster was growing up and he was being weaned on fish. The seal was still fond of milk, but there were other ways of giving it to him.

The boy took the shining milk pail from its shelf in the kitchen and went out, whistling.

In the box on the porch Buster raised himself on his little front flippers as he bobbed his head up and down, barking his eager "Good morning."

"Rise and shine!" Clint told him. "Hit the deck!"

Buster raised himself higher, slid over the edge of the box, and rocked across the porch and down the steps at Clint's heels. At that moment Wolf and Jerry came bounding around the house, barking their greetings.

It had happened so many times they all knew just what to do. Clint put the milk pail down on the porch and petted and wrestled with the dogs and the seal. Sometimes in the free-for-all, Wolf or Jerry would growl at Buster and pretend to bite him; and Buster would turn his head, quick as a snake, barking and snapping back. But no one got bit.

The first time the dogs had caught Buster outdoors they had ganged up on him; but Buster had backed into a corner between the steps and porch and defended himself so valiantly that the dogs were discouraged by the time Clint's mother came to drive them away. After that they became friends. Buster held no grudge against the dogs, and he had so much of a puppy's good nature and playfulness that they accepted him as one of them.

The tussle ended and Wolf and Jerry got out of the way as Clint turned on the hose.

"Time for a shower, Buster!"

The seal rocked happily as the water darkened his mottled gray coat. He would have stayed under the hose all day, but time was short.

"Face-wash, Buster!"

Buster held still and looked down his nose while Clint sprayed his sleek head and whiskered face.

"Funny old Buster. Anyone that fond of a shower ought to like a real bath!"

Clint found that when the seal was dry for too long the oily film over his eyes gummed up and bothered him. Maybe Buster's eyes remembered the ocean. But not Buster! Sunday morning Clint had taken him to the edge of the beach and was urging him into a few inches of water when a wave from a passing cruiser slopped over him. Buster gave a loud snort and headed for the house. And he couldn't be coaxed back.

"Time for milking!" Clint turned off the water, took up the pail and went to the barn, with Wolf and Jerry trotting ahead and Buster rocking alongside, talking in eager little whines and barks. Clint knew in a general way what Buster was saying:

"It's a good morning, and I had a good shower, and we're off to the barn for milk.

Let's hurry and get it while it's warm!"

When they reached the barn the dogs lost interest and went to prowl around outside; Buster, eager and excited, followed Clint inside. Milking with his head against Juno's flank, Clint could see Buster out of the corner of his eye—begging to send some his way.

"All right, Buster." Clint turned one of the teats outward. "Here it is, air line!" The white stream curved through the dusk of the barn and into Buster's waiting mouth.

"That's enough now," Clint said as he turned the stream back into the pail.

Buster held his pose awhile, with drops of milk on his whiskers. Then he began coaxing again.

"Wait your turn," Clint told him. "You're not going to get it all!"

When the pail was three-quarters full, Clint turned one of the teats outward and upward again.

"Ready, Buster!"

The seal's head was up again and his neck wove from side to side as he fielded the swaying stream of milk.

On the way back to the house Buster walloped along happily beside Clint, telling with little barks and whines what a successful expedition they had had, and coaxing for more.

"I told you before, it's a school day," Clint said. "Wait till Saturday. I'm going to give you another swimming lesson. You're a big boy now, and shower baths are kid stuff. It's getting warm enough for me to go swimming, too. We'll have fun!"

Clint's mother no longer allowed Buster in the house. He had a way of getting into things. And when she was hurrying from one room to another, he liked to set his teeth in the hem of her dress and be towed along. In general, though, he got along with the family as well as Clint had hoped. And if he was a nuisance at times, he made up for it by his good nature and by the playful things he did.

At breakfast Clint heard him wallop softly along the porch and come to a stop beneath the window. There were light butting and scuffling and scratching sounds as Buster worked himself upright against the clapboards. Then his funny whiskered face looked in while his flippers held onto the window sill.

Clint watched out of the corner of his eye, pretending not to notice. Buster tightened his hold with one flipper, and raised the other to knock cautiously against the glass. Clint turned as if he had just noticed the seal, and Buster's face lighted up and he whined and coaxed and gestured to Clint.

Mom laughed. "He's asking you to come out and play, just like any youngster."

On the way up the trail to the school bus, Clint thought of one more thing about seals. They had descended from animals that resembled bears, and probably were once just as surly—yet even grown-up seals were friendly and playful if people gave them a chance. There must be a reason for that friendly sea change, but the books didn't say anything about it.

Next day Clint woke with a feeling that the spring morning would never end and he could enjoy it forever if he chose. He dressed at the open window that looked out on the wide, quiet arm of the sea, silver between dark shores and touched with mist. Into the room there came the smell of dew and growing things, and the iodine tang of the shore.

The good spring smell followed him downstairs, where a fire was snapping and roaring in the kitchen range. The coffeepot was on, and his father was sitting at the table figuring on the back of an envelope.

He looked up briefly as Clint came in. "Morning, boy."

"Good morning, Dad." He wanted to say something about the morning, but his father was going to camp early and he had other things on his mind.

As Clint went out with the milk pail Buster raised up in his box and the dogs came bounding round the corner of the house. But today Buster romped lazily, and after his shower he rocked back up the steps to his box as if he had lost some sleep and were going to find it.

The boy went on to the barn with the dogs. The spring made him dreamy and he milked mechanically, thinking of other things, until the milk ceased coming. He was surprised to be done so quickly, and even more surprised when he saw barely a quart of milk in the bottom of the pail.

"That won't do, Juno," he said. "You'll have to give."

He commenced milking again, but got only a few squirts. Juno moved restlessly and raised a threatening left hind hoof, as if she wanted to kick him for not being able to take a hint.

"Have it your way." He got up hastily and carried the almost empty pail to the house. It was a mystery, and Clint thought all mysteries interesting because they were something to solve. His father didn't see it that way.

"A cow doesn't go dry overnight, Clint! Better go back and finish milking."

"There isn't any more, Dad. I kept on until Juno started to kick me."

"Sure you didn't feed the rest to that seal of yours?"

"Buster wasn't even there!"

His father was about to go to the barn and try for himself. Then he gestured for Clint to take the pail away.

"I'll do the milking myself next time. Now get on with your chores."

When Clint went out again the freshness was gone from the morning. His father had as good as said that he didn't know how to milk a cow—and he had done his best! Well, let Dad try!

That evening his father did the milking and he came in with a brimming pailful.

"Juno hasn't gone dry yet, boy!" There wasn't any harshness in his voice. And he had said "boy"; Clint knew then that everything was all right.

"I'm glad of that, Dad. Juno sure had me guessing!"

He promised himself that next morning he would get as much milk as his father

38

had. He was up and dressed on time, but when he went for the pail it was gone; and Buster was gone from his box. Clint went alone to feed the chickens. At least he was trusted to do that!

On his way to the chicken yard his father called from the barn.

"Clint, come here a minute!"

He came on the run. His father was at the open door with the milk pail in his hand. He motioned toward the barn.

"Take a look in there!"

There was Buster, on the milking side of Juno, raised on his front flippers and nursing greedily and making little whines of contentment.

It was Clint who slapped Buster and drove him out of the barn.

But the seal didn't take the lesson to heart. He accepted being slapped and hustled out as he did the morning tussle on the grass, and on the way to the house he frolicked along beside Clint, talking eagerly.

Clint wasn't listening. He was thinking how he was going to fix the barn door as soon as he got home from school. The lower hinge was loose and some of the wood was broken away from the other side. It was only a little piece, but it was enough for

Buster to get his nose in and squeeze his streamlined shape through.

The door could be fixed with half an hour's work. But now there would be other things to look out for. Buster was intelligent and active and full of fun—the way seals should be. But a seal that was intelligent enough to go to the barn and milk a cow was sure to think of other things that would get him into mischief.

4. THE SISSY SEAL

SCHOOL was out, and Clint's friends from Big River paid one of their rare visits to Barlow's Landing. They arrived a little before noon, in the Deckers' boat with the old two-horse outboard.

Clint and Buster were waiting on the beach as the boys came in: Len Decker, who was a year older than Clint, with his young brother Phil; and George Lawson, who was Len's age, but smaller and quieter.

The Deckers and Lawsons farmed on the

river delta to the north; Clint hardly ever saw the boys except at school. They worked week ends and summers. When they had finished high school they were going to settle down on the farm; their lives were already decided. Sometimes Clint envied them, other times he didn't. But he always felt that he was on the outside, because they knew just what they were going to do.

As the boat came in to the beach, Len shut off the motor, tilted it, and shouted:

"Hi, Clint! About tired of waiting for us?"

Phil called in a thin voice:

"Is that your seal, Clint? Gee, he's nice!"

George Lawson gave Clint a friendly salute.

They piled out, dressed in blue jeans and cotton shirts, and old sneakers; their leather jackets and sweaters were in the boat. Len carried a twenty-two rifle, and all of them had sandwiches in paper bags.

"We were going to get here early," Len said, "but my old man made me finish plowing."

Phil was making friends with Buster, who was barking at him. His voice sounded friendly, but he was saying as clearly as words that he didn't yet know the boy.

"He's sure nice," Phil said. "If I had a seal I wouldn't want anything else!"

"You would, too," Len told him. "Anyway, the folks wouldn't let you keep it. Seals get to be nuisances." Len was taller than Clint, but heavy-set, so he seemed short. His red face was half-friendly, half-suspicious. He looked around the beach, and south toward the point. "First we'll figure where we're going to eat."

Clint told him, "Mom is expecting us to eat at the house."

"Gee!"

"That's nice of her."

Len shook his head. "With sandwiches we can eat when we like. Maybe we'll be going swimming, and we don't want to wait an hour after chow."

"It's too cold for swimming," Phil said.

"Not for me," Len told his brother. "And we're going to see Buster's first swim; that's what we came for." He looked at Clint with his laughing, suspicious eyes. "You haven't been giving him swimming lessons, have you?"

"He's never been in the water in his life, except under the hose."

"Let's go to Pleasant Harbor and laze around there," Len decided. "Fish for pogies, maybe; we got lines in the boat.

43

Maybe go swimming; and have our chow
when we like. Buster can do his stuff there.
I bet when he gets in the water he'll go
like he was jet-propelled!"

They all agreed that Pleasant Harbor was
the right place. It was only half a mile
long and a few hundred yards wide, like a
mountain lake, with steep shores covered
with fir trees. No one lived there except
at the far end, where the shore was low
and damp. At the edge of the woods there
were a few cabins where fishermen holed
up for the winter. Halfway along the west
shore there was the log dump and boom
where Clint's father dumped his logs. Just
inside the harbor there was a high sand bar;
and in the little bay behind it a float went
out into deep water.

Clint's mother sent along fried chicken
and a picnic cake and milk. The boys and
Buster ate on the float. The seal's fish appetite was always good, but he was nervous about having the water so close; and at
first he stayed near Clint, looking worried
—as if he wanted Clint to take the sea
away.

After lunch the boys told each other it
was warm enough to go swimming. They
talked about whether they were supposed
to wait half an hour, or an hour. The hour

passed without their getting any farther
than talking about it as they lay on the
float in the afternoon sun, fishing for
pogies.

The tide was going out, and the pogies
wouldn't bite; they were as well fed as the
boys. Now and then one of them looked at
the bait—like Phil looking at the remaining
pieces of cake—and turned its head away.
It was fun just to see them there in the
green water, with a crab moving on the
sand below, or a streamer of sea lettuce
fluttering in the current. . . .

Clint was roused by the sharp crack of
the twenty-two.

Len was shooting at a cork float drifting
out toward the entrance of the harbor; the
other boys were taking in their lines. No
one had caught anything but bullheads,
which Buster had eaten, and there was no
bait on Clint's hook. He didn't know how
long it had been that way. And the bait
that had been beside him on the float was
gone; Buster had eaten it.

Out in the harbor the floating cork
jumped from the shock of a bullet. "Got
him!" Len said.

George took off his water-soaked bait, and
sank the hook deep in the cedar chip on
which his line was wound.

"Don't leave any bait on your hook," he told Phil. "Buster would get stuck with it."

Len shot again, and missed. "Who's going in?"

There were no answering cheers. Phil put one foot in the water, and pulled it back quickly.

"Ouch!"

"Baby!" Len started to take off his clothes. "Last one in is a cream puff!"

The boys all began undressing, without much enthusiasm. Clint was pulling his undershirt off over his head when he heard Len plunge in. Icy water splashed over him. Buster whimpered, and bumped against his legs. Clint thought it was the sudden noise that bothered him.

Len came up, blowing, and caught the edge of the float.

"Wow! I jumped into the deep freeze all right!" Then he kicked off from the float and swam away under water.

George went in next; then Phil followed with a yell, and swam away. Clint took a deep breath and dived from the edge of the float. After the first shock it wasn't so bad. He swam down, resolutely, to the bottom and held on for a few seconds, watching a big red sea cucumber feeding itself with its fifteen branched tentacles.

When Clint surfaced and shook the wet hair out of his eyes, he saw Phil back on the float, shivering into his clothes. George was holding onto the edge of the float as if he were about to get out; and Len was treading water a little way off, calling them cream puffs and saying the water was fine. But in another minute they were all out, and Buster was frisking happily because the foolishness was over. Len looked at him sourly.

"Hey, we came here to see Buster's swimming lesson. How about it, Clint?"

"Sure," Clint said, "as soon as I figure out how we're going to work it."

"Push him off the float, of course!"

"No, he might drown, or inhale enough water to get pneumonia."

"For crying out loud! Don't kid me that seals can't swim!"

"I'm not kidding. If a baby seal falls in the water it can drown unless its mother helps it. She holds it up from underneath, and pushes it ashore."

"You and your books! I say push him off; he'll swim like he was jet-propelled!"

George suggested, "Let's try him in shallow water, near shore."

"Like a baby pool," Phil said.

47

"Yah, a baby pool! Well, bring him over and throw him in!"

Clint stopped where the water was about two feet deep.

"We won't throw him in," he said. "I'll get in the water; and the rest of you kind of lower him down, and I'll hold up his chin."

"For crying out loud!"

To Clint it was an exciting event—repeating something that had happened millions of years ago: the land animal going back to the sea.

Buster didn't want to go back. He tried to coax Clint out of the knee-deep water; but he couldn't be coaxed in, and he didn't want to be lifted.

Everyone had a hand in the launching of Buster. George joined Clint in the water, ready to help with the seal's rear end while Clint held up his chin; Len, who had wanted to push him off from the first, was to get him over the edge of the float to the boys in the water; and Phil, whom Buster trusted more than Len, was to stand at his head and quiet him.

"Ready?" Len asked.

"Ready. Take it easy."

"Nice Buster."

"That's a boy, Buster; I'll hold up your chin."

They lifted him off quite easily after all, and lowered him into the water. Buster's big eyes looked up anxiously as Clint let his forward end down into a swimming position, with his nose just above the surface.

"There you are, nice Bust—"

There was a loud snort as Buster exploded into action, knocking Clint over backward in one direction, and George in another. Sitting in the mud, with his head just above the surface, Clint saw Buster flounder out of the shallow water, and ashore. Muddy and shivering, with his hand cut by a shell, Clint stood on the float and watched him rock up the slope of the sand bar.

Len's mouth was still open.

"What happened?"

"Everything!" Phil said.

Clint explained, "He got some water up his nose—"

"For crying out loud! A seal, and he couldn't take it!"

"A cream puff!"

"A sissy seal!"

Clint's ears burned as he started after Buster. He was still a land animal.

5. RETURN TO THE SEA

THE crackling fire in the range still sounded good as it drove the night's chill from the kitchen, but outside there was a fresh new warmth at sunrise.

Buster, who helped Clint with everything but the milking, approved of summer. He never seemed to tire of showing how pleased he was that the boy had got over his bad habit of going to school five mornings a week.

Now they ate breakfast in full daylight;

the three of them—or was it four? This
morning Buster was on the porch just outside, holding onto the sill with his flippers
with his fun-loving face looking in the window. It was almost as if he were in a chair
at the far end of the table.

Dad looked at the kitchen clock, and
turned on the radio. After a few seconds
an announcer's voice came in pleasantly:

*Fair today and tomorrow, with light west-
erly winds. Temperature at six A.M., sixty
degrees. Humidity, sixty . . .*

It didn't take a broadcasting station to
tell that it was going to be a wonderful
day; but there could be such a thing as too
fine weather. When the humidity was low
the ground cover in the woods dried out,
there was danger of forest fires, and logging camps were shut down. Sixty degrees
humidity was better than safe.

"Not bad," Clint's father said. "With luck
we'll finish logging that forty." He turned
to shut off the radio, then hesitated as
music poured into the kitchen.

"Leave it on," Mom said. "It's 'The Dance
of the Hours.' I've always liked it."

"Somebody else likes it, too," Dad said.
"Look!"

Outside the window Buster was swaying
his raised head in time to the music.

51

"He might be leading an orchestra!" Mom said.

Buster's funny seal face had the look of an old master, and he swayed to the music as if he were dancing with the hours—hours filled with summer and romping with boys and dogs.

When the music ended, Buster waited a few moments, then rapped on the window with the knuckles of his right flipper, asking for more. But the next thing on the radio was a commercial, and Dad turned it off.

Buster rapped again, and Clint shook his head at him. "No more."

The seal made a silly, despairing face, and dropped out of sight below the window.

Clint's father laughed as they all got up from the table.

"Your seal may never be a swimmer, boy, but maybe he'll learn to play the fiddle or something!"

"Seals are supposed to be musical," Clint said. "I've read that in England they used to come up out of the Channel on Sunday mornings, and listen to the church bells."

"That was right Christian of them." Dad smiled. "You know, there is something Christian-looking about seals—even if they are so full of mischief."

52

It seemed a good time to ask, and Clint followed his father out to the front porch, where he changed from house slippers or shoes to steel-calked logger's boots. That morning, beyond the land, there was a wide expanse of wet sand and gravel and seaweed; and the boats were far up the beach from the shrunken water. It was the lowest tide of summer, and it invited an expedition.

"Dad, I think I could get some geoducks. We won't have tide like this for a long time. Would it be all right if I went before I did the hoeing? I can't start anyway until the dew is off—"

His father was smiling as he sat on the edge of the porch, lacing a boot.

"You've more reasons than a lawyer, boy! Go ahead, if your mother doesn't need you —and don't let Buster fall in!"

On their way to the beach Clint explained the plan of action to the seal.

"The *Dolphin* is too heavy to launch on this tide. There's no wind, anyway. So we'll take the little skiff. We'll go to the Flats; and if you're good I'll dig some clams for you. Don't snort around and scare the geoducks—you don't even know what they are, but I'll show you. It's pronounced 'gooeyduck,' but you wouldn't know it by the spelling."

When he had the skiff at the water's edge, Clint explained one more thing to the seal.

"You heard what Dad said about not letting you fall in. You ought to be ashamed. A big seal like you afraid of salt water! We're going to have a swimming lesson at the Flats, and if you don't learn I'll get you an inner tube!"

Buster pranced his head and whined in happy agreement.

"I hope you mean it," Clint said. "Now, get in." He tipped the skiff toward Buster, who floundered over the gunwale midships, where he could get in from the beach.

At ordinary low tides the Flats extended half a mile beyond the land. Now, with a minus tide, they looked like a continent that had just risen from the sea, still wet, and dim with the light morning mist.

Clint brought the skiff in silently, out of respect for a newly discovered world. Over his shoulder he saw the tall silhouette of a heron on the shore, like a shadow cast on the mist.

"S-h-h-h-h, Buster!"

The seal could be noisy enough at home; but Clint hadn't had to teach him much about being quiet on expeditions. Buster was motionless in the bottom of the boat, looking up at the boy like a happy conspirator.

Looking over his shoulder again, Clint saw the heron less than fifty feet away, beginning to show the first signs of uneasiness. The keel grated lightly on shells in the mud. There was a hoarse squawk, and the heron flapped into the air, swinging up his long legs and trailing them behind him as he faded into the mist.

"We've scared the inhabitants away," Clint said. "We might as well go ashore. That was a great blue heron, by the way; a male. You can tell by the crest on the back of his head."

He stepped out into mud and water, and pulled the boat up, high but not dry.

"All ashore, Buster!" He tipped the skiff for the seal, who looked eagerly at Clint, then doubtfully at the muddy beach.

"It's the best we have, Buster. All ashore!"

Buster flopped out, and Clint took up the clam shovel and bucket.

"We'll try our luck this way."

They went toward the point, where the wide Flats dropped off into four hundred feet of water.

"S-h-h-h-h!"

Buster stopped beside Clint, and they listened to the sound from the deep water off the point: the hoarse, powerful breathing of invisible swimmers.

"Know what that is?"

Buster didn't.

"Seals."

That didn't mean anything to him, either.

"Wait and see."

They waited, and two dark heads appeared through the mist on the water, and drew abreast of them.

The seals passed like powerful swimmers who knew where they were going and wouldn't get tired on the way. They kept near each other, like friends, and their loud breathing seemed to be something they did for fun, or talking; there wasn't any feeling of effort.

"Your seals are good people," Clint said.

Buster looked, politely, but he would have been more interested in boys or dogs to wrestle with, or a radio to listen to.

They went on, with Clint studying the beach. Clams squirted around his feet; and he passed horse clams, with the wrinkled, inch-thick ends of their siphons level with the sand. A geyser of water shot up beside his foot, drenching his leg to the knee.

"Heck!" He stepped back, frowning at the

smooth hole in the sand, with his foot-
print touching it. "That was a geoduck,
Buster. Must have been a piece of seaweed
over his siphon, and I stepped on him.
He's gone now, and we aren't going to dig
to China for him!"

They went on more carefully, and
stopped near a siphon end in the sand. It
wasn't any thicker than the siphon of a big
horse clam; but instead of being wrinkled,
it was smooth.

"This is it, Buster. Now, *s-h-h-h!*"

The seal shushed, and Clint went to work.

There are half a dozen ways of digging a
geoduck, with people to swear by all of
them. Clint believed five of them were
wrong, because they were illegal, or scared
the geoduck into sounding. The right way
was the one he had learned from the Indians. He dug down carefully a foot away
from the siphon. People who never tried it
said you couldn't dig that close, but you
could.

Clint hadn't been able to find much about
the geoduck's habits in books; but he had
studied them, and written a class paper
about them. He said they had one-dimensional lives and instincts. All their motions
were vertical: putting their siphons up to
the surface to feed, and pulling them down

when they were alarmed. And they tried to dig themselves deeper when someone was after them; but they didn't get far. Usually the geoduck was only a few inches above stones Clint's foot couldn't move.

The geoduck's sense of danger was also one-dimensional, Clint had written. He was alert to disturbances near the end of his siphon, but he paid no attention to digging that went on beside him. He accepted it as some other mollusk going about his business—or he didn't know it was happening because it was happening in a dimension outside his life.

Clint had written the paper for English, because he didn't want to write about "What I Saw on My Trip to Town." Some of the class had liked the paper; but most of them said it had too many big words. At noon, and for a week afterward, Len Decker made fun of him and said Clint thought himself too good for the class. Clint was sorry he had turned in the paper; but by writing it he had found out what he knew about geoducks, and what he didn't.

When Clint had finished, the hole was a foot-and-a-half deep, sloping in from the far side; and between the geoduck and the hole there was a straight wall of sand and gravel about a foot thick.

"Now, Buster, we'll see if our calculations are right."

Buster looked up from nosing a transparent ghost shrimp that had been dug out of its burrow, and pranced his head to say that their calculations were wonderful.

"Wait, Buster, we haven't got him yet. First we go like this . . ." He began digging under the wall between the hole and the geoduck, feeling the shovel's way through sand and gravel while he kept an eye on the unsuspecting siphon.

"S-h-h-h, Buster. A few more inches—"

The shovel grated harshly on a stone—and a fountain of clear water shot up as the siphon end disappeared. Clint drove the shovel forward with all his strength. As it stopped he felt something alive bump down on the steel blade.

"There we are, Buster."

There wasn't much to see: the sloping handle of the shovel disappearing into mud and water that stirred with disturbed ghost shrimp.

With his hands Clint crumbled away the wall, uncovering the cream and white shape of the huge clam, still vertical, like its life. He lifted it out by its foot-long siphon, and hefted it.

"Nice one, Buster; it'll weigh five pounds."

The geoduck's siphon was twice too long to go inside its heavy, almost square shell; and its thick mantle bulged out in front for all the world as if it had bought its coat in the children's department. There just wasn't enough shell to do what was originally intended.

The books didn't say whether the geoduck dug itself in deep to protect its exposed parts, or whether its shell had got careless when there wasn't so much need for it. Or why geoducks were found in only two small areas in the world. One was Puget Sound, and the other was the African Coast, thousands of miles away. It seemed to Clint that someone should try to find out why such different places seemed alike to a prehistoric clam.

He stopped after the second geoduck, and dug some butter clams, which he opened for the seal.

"You've been a good boy, Buster."

Buster barked something like, "The same to you," and coaxed the boy to go on with him and explore the world they had discovered by themselves.

When they turned back, the tide was

coming in strongly; the skiff was afloat, and the anchor was under water.

"Careless of us, Buster. We'll have to wade, or maybe swim for it. That is, I'll swim. You wouldn't know about things like that!"

The anchor was a long way out; but with the easy slope of the beach he got to it in water a little above his knees. When he had pulled the boat up to himself and stowed the shovel and bucket, he looked back and saw Buster fretting at the edge of the rising water, lifting one flipper and then the other, barking to Clint to come back to him out of the wet and dangerous stuff.

"The heck I will!" Clint called. "You come here!"

Buster's answer sounded as if he were saying he would go through fire for Clint. But deep salt water—he had to draw the line somewhere!

"Here, Buster! Come on, Buster!" It had started as a game, but Clint had changed the strategy. Buster wouldn't come toward him, and he was too worried to retreat. While he stayed where he was, coaxing the boy to come back, the tide rose around him. Now, as he raised alternate flippers, they sloshed like the paddles of a rolling side-wheel steamer.

"Here, Buster! Come on, Buster!"

The seal was almost afloat now. It seemed to Clint that it was the deciding moment of both their lives.

"Here, Buster! Here, Buster—"

There was a loud snort as if the seal had got some water up his nose.

"Buster, here, Buster! Come on!"

There was another snort—and Buster was gliding toward him, with his head raised proudly.

Clint, standing in water to his waist, cheered.

"Buster, you've done it!"

The seal glided up to him, with a proud, happy look; he seemed to be smiling all over his face. Clint was, too. Buster's own mother couldn't have been as proud.

"Buster, you've done it! You're swimming!"

Buster came almost close enough to touch, with a gleam of mischief in his eyes. Suddenly he ducked his head, and with a smooth lunge he glided away under the surface.

Clint scrambled over the stern of the skiff. A hundred feet away, in deep water, Buster's sleek head popped above the surface. Clint was stowing the anchor when Buster came swimming alongside, with his new, proud, happy look.

"Here, Buster, come around to the stern and I'll help you in."

Buster dived, and was gone again.

Clint started to row home alone. He was proud of Buster, but he had an empty feeling; and he wondered what he had done with himself before he found the little seal on the beach.

He stopped rowing when Buster came swimming toward him, only to dive again. Looking down, Clint saw him zoom by, like a flying shadow.

The seal had passed his swimming teacher forever. He had become one of the mysteries of the undersea tides that he explored, while Clint could only look in from the surface.

6. THE MEN'S WORLD

Clint's mother was in Seattle for a week,
visiting Aunt Harriet, and Clint was in
charge at home. Things weren't as neat as
his mother kept them; but Clint and his
father got along, and housekeeping didn't
take much time.

Mom would have spent half an hour fixing lunch. Clint just put a hamburger on
and let it fry while he washed the dishes,
which had been soaking since morning. He
had the radio on for Buster, who was in

the middle of the kitchen floor, swaying in time to the "Blue Danube" waltz.

When Buster had become a great swimmer, Clint had feared it would end their companionship. Instead it had been more like a beginning. On these summer days they were together almost all the time from sunrise to late dark.

Before Buster had taken to the water Clint had been a little sorry for him, crippling around on land. Now maybe Buster was sorry for the boy.

The waltz ended, and the seal whined coaxingly for more.

"Time to eat, Buster."

When Clint had turned off the radio, he put his hamburger in a bun, piled on pickle relish, and poured himself a glass of milk. Buster didn't get his big meal until evening, but Clint put a few chunks of raw fish on the plate for him.

As the seal walloped down the steps beside him, the boy reminded him, "When Mom comes home, remember, you aren't allowed in the house."

They ate under the Gravenstein apple tree in the yard. Buster's fish went in half a dozen bites. After that he raised his head as high as he could, and begged. Next, he whined, then barked coaxingly. Clint showed his empty hands, and shook his head.

"No more!"

Buster gave a despairing look and toppled over, pretending to drop dead. It wasn't anything Clint had taught him; he was a born comedian.

Clint sprawled on the grass, looking up at a patch of blue among the thick leaves of the apple tree and listening to the drowsy hum of bees. Buster came walloping over to him, and he sat up to escape a seal kiss.

Buster edged in the direction of the water, barking and whining and looking over his shoulder at the boy.

"No, Buster. No swimming for half an hour. We've just had lunch."

Buster raised his head with a look that said, "What, no swimming?"

"Not now. First we have to take a nap. Here, Buster!" He patted the ground beside him.

Buster came over and settled down, and Clint lay back with his head resting on the seal. You'd expect a seal to smell fishy, but Buster didn't have any smell and he made a nice springy pillow. The boy propped one leg on the other knee and wiggled his bare toes against the sky.

"This is the life, Buster!"

There was a blue haze over the distant land, and on the miles of water there was only one boat, with its sails reflecting white in the still channel.

"Summer," Clint said to Buster, "is something we ought to have more of. I'll tell you what we'll do. One of these times we'll go exploring in the *Dolphin* for a whole week, maybe. No coming home at night. I'll take the sleeping bag and you'll take what you've got on. We won't take any food—just fishing tackle and a clam shovel and an oyster knife. We'll live off the land and the water."

Buster shifted his position, then was quiet again. Clint went on:

"I can get along just as well as you can, Buster; you'll see. If we're not smart enough to find any other food, we'll live on plankton."

Buster gave a little bark of agreement.

"We'll go everywhere—to Big River to see the boys; and we'll visit old Tim Walsh in his floathouse at Triton Cove. Tim's a hundred years old, and full of stories. And we'll go to Lynch Cove; it's warm and shallow there; maybe we'll find some new specimens."

Clint's daydreaming was ended by his

pillow getting up to shake itself and to remind him about swimming.

"All right, Buster." Clint got up and started toward the beach. "But just a short one; we have work to do."

A short swim meant out to the float and back, with a little horsing around on the float. They raced as usual; Buster paddled out slowly beside Clint, who waded until the water was deep enough.

"Ready?"

Buster whined that he was ready any time.

Clint lunged forward in the water, his right arm out for the crawl. Before he could make a stroke, Buster was zooming away ahead. When Clint was halfway to the float, he met Buster coming back.

"You win," Clint told him. "You always do."

Buster came toward him until it looked as if they would have a head-on collision; then he dived suddenly. Clint felt the powerful lunge when the seal passed under him. As he neared the float, Buster popped up beside him, with a delighted look on his face. He swam slowly, and together they climbed up on the float, where the seal barked excitedly to announce that they had got there at the same time.

When they dived, Clint swam down toward a spotted sole that was resting on the sand. A flying shadow that was Buster flashed by below him. Presently Clint came up again; he held on to the side of the float while he filled his lungs with air and scrambled out into the sunshine. It was summer air, but the water was cold.

Fifty yards away Buster rose in the water like a cork and looked around for Clint. When he saw him, he came charging toward the float.

"What's the matter?" he seemed to ask. "I thought you were going in."

"I'm not in your class, Buster," Clint said as the seal scrambled out. "You could give me swimming lessons, but you can't give me flippers."

Buster would have spent the rest of the day diving from the float, but there were other things to do.

"No more," Clint told him. "The next dive is toward home, and I'll race you. Ready!"

Buster was ready, drawn together like a padded spring.

"Go!"

Clint's shallow dive was slanted toward shore; but while he was still in the air he heard Buster's smooth-powered lunge going away from him. When he was halfway to shore, Buster came to swim beside him and make the race a tie.

In the warm air, Clint felt a tingling glow that the seal probably had all the time he was in the water. On land, there were things Clint understood better than Buster.

"Back to splitting shakes," he announced when he had his clothes on. "How else do you suppose we'll get a roof on the new chicken house?"

Buster didn't know.

Splitting shakes was a job Clint liked. It wasn't work when you knew how to do it. All you needed was a froe and a mallet— and shake bolts, of course. Shake bolts are blocks of cedar about three feet long, and there was a heap of them under the king apple tree by the woodshed, where Clint's father had dumped them out of the truck.

Clint upended one of the bolts and took up the froe and the mallet. A froe is a straight steel blade with an upright wooden handle at one end. He set the sharp blade half an inch from the edge of the bolt, across the grain, and struck the back with the mallet. *Whang!* An even half-inch slab flew off the bolt. All it needed was a hint, and it turned into a shake—light, and strong, and good for fifty years. Again Clint set the blade and struck with the mallet.

Whang! There was the next shake. *Whang!*
Whang! And the next, and the next.

As he whanged away, setting up a new
bolt when the old one was used up, the
shakes piled up around him and their fra-
grance mingled with the summer air. Clint
paused to kick some of them out of the way
before setting up a new bolt.

"Buster, you lazy seal, you ought to be
moving this stuff out of my way so I can
work."

Buster came over from the far side of
the apple tree. He had nothing against
shakes; but Clint had kicked them, so they
must be the enemy. He took one in his
sharp teeth and toted it back to his place,
where he settled down to chew it. His look
was like a question.

"Is this the one you don't like?"

"Not that one, Buster; this one." He
pointed to another shake, and Buster got
up and carried it under the tree. It showed
intelligence, and it gave Clint an idea. Buster wanted to help; why shouldn't he?

"That one, too." He indicated another
shake, and Buster took it and put it with
the first two, then looked up for orders.

"Another one," Clint told him. "All of
them."

Buster came back for another, and another; after a little more coaching he was continuing without any bossing. It was the first time he had helped with work, and he rocked back and forth proudly, carrying shakes from one pile to another.

With Buster helping, it was less work than ever. Each shake flew off the bolt as if it had been waiting to do that. It was doing what was natural to it; cedar was made to split.

Old Tim said cedar was the complete tree; the Indians wouldn't have had much of a life without it. Out of split-cedar boards they made houses—some of them nearly a quarter of a mile long, with apartments for dozens of families. They made canoes out of cedar logs, and fishing lines and nets out of the twisted bark of young cedar; and they used pounded bark to make light summer clothes. They used shredded cedar bark for tinder; they could carry fire great distances by putting a smoldering wad of bark in a split stick. With the salmon they caught by cedar nets and lines, the Indians had everything they needed.

Cedar had helped white men in almost as many ways as it had the Indians; and the best music in the world was Puget Sound rain on cedar-roof shakes.

Buster tired of work after a while and

rested under the apple tree. Late in the afternoon he began coaxing for another swim, and Clint laid aside his mallet and froe.

"Just a short one, Buster. It's almost time to start supper. What are you going to have, fish?"

"Fish" was a word Buster understood. He barked and nodded his head, to say fish would be fine with him—but they mustn't let anything interfere with their swim.

After their swim they went to start supper. In the kitchen Clint turned on a music program. While the range heated, he set the table, peeled potatoes, fixed Kentucky Wonder beans, and husked corn from the garden. Then he put the baked ham in the oven to heat.

Clint wasn't a fancy cook, but he made out all right with everything but desserts— his mother knew that, and she had baked pies before she left.

It was good to have Mom, and it was good in a different way when she wasn't there. Half-forgotten things seemed to come out of corners and start building a different world. It was a men's world.

Over a third cup of coffee and his pipe Clint's father talked about Alaska.

"Alaska's a man's country," he said.

"Women find it too lonesome. Your Aunt Harriet wouldn't like the wilderness, or any of the towns the way they are—but maybe she'd like trying to change them. That would keep her busy. About your Ma, I don't know. If we could take our home along, she might like it all right. Sometimes, in this kind of weather, I think about taking another shot at Alaska. We'd build our own boat, here on the beach—"

Clint said, "I could help you a lot!"

His father nodded. "We'd build a boat big enough to live on. I think your Ma would be satisfied if her housekeeping wasn't upset; she'd probably get to like it. We'd lie up in the mouth of one of the rivers in Southeastern, and fish and hunt and prospect—"

Clint said, "I'd learn more than I would at school."

His father went on, "Prospecting's fun, even if you don't find gold. The time I was there three of us spent the summer on Johnson River. We didn't find what we went after, but every day was exciting—"

The boy refilled his father's coffee cup.

"Lots of gold had been taken out of the sand at the mouth of the river, but it had played out and nobody bothered with it any more. We didn't figure it that way. We

said, 'The gold came from somewhere up-
stream. It maybe took a thousand years for
it to wash down to the mouth. We'll go up
the river and find the gold-bearing gravel it
came from. . . .' "

"That was using brains!" Clint said.

Dad answered with a slow grin. "We
thought so. We panned our way clear to the
head of the river in the mountains. It took
us all summer, and we found one color
of gold—about thirty cents' worth. In the
fall the others went back to the States, and
I got a job in a machine shop in Ketchikan.
But there isn't much in working for other
people; next year I came home on a fishing
boat. That's the story of the Johnson River
expedition."

"It sounded like a good idea," Clint said.
"When we go up there in our boat we'll
try some other place."

"No, we'll go back to Johnson River."

Clint stared in surprise. "But you didn't
find anything—"

"Look, boy." His father drew pencil lines
on an envelope.

"Here's the river bed, like a trough.
Here's the river, at the bottom. It wasn't
always down there—I got to thinking about
it the other day. It took thousands of years
to cut down through gravel and rock. May-

be a thousand years ago the river was up here, cutting through gold-bearing gravel; carrying gold downstream. When it cut deeper it didn't bring down any more—"

Clint broke in, "And the gold vein is up in the riverbank!"

"Maybe," his father agreed. "It could be that we went along the river bed like people looking for windfalls in an orchard— when all the time there were trees full of apples overhead."

"Let's start the boat this fall," Clint said. "I'll split more shakes and build a shed where we can work all winter, and—"

"Easy, boy, there are lots of things to think about first."

"But the gold is there, Dad! You can't be wrong—" He was stopped by the twinkle in his father's sea-blue eyes.

"It's the easiest thing in the world—being wrong. There are so many ways of doing it. When the three of us went up there we had it all figured out—"

"But you left out one step!"

"Maybe we're leaving out two now. I'd like to have a shot at it, but if we go it'll be when we can afford it." He got up, knocking the ashes from his pipe into the geoduck shell he used for an ash tray.

"We'll plan to have fun even if we never see a color of gold."

As the boy cleared away the dishes it seemed to him that the gold of the Johnson River had been almost close enough to touch. It was fading now, but someday they would go after it and make it real again.

7. KILLER WHALES

THE school bus stopped at the mailbox
with JAMES BARLOW printed on the
side, and Clint got out into the pouring
rain.

"Don't get your feet wet!" Len Decker
called after him.

George Lawson raised his hand in his
usual friendly salute.

Then the door closed and the bus went
on as Clint started down the hill toward the
house.

From the road, all you could see of the Barlow place were the wet shake roofs of farm buildings and the bare orchard with a few dozen forgotten yellow apples on a Bellflower tree. Orchard and land and roofs looked wetter than the gray plain of water beyond them. But smoke from the kitchen chimney was wrestling with the rain. Inside it would be warm and dry, with good cooking smells.

Going back to school hadn't turned out as bad as Clint had feared. The worst part had been worrying about what might happen to Buster while he was away. He had told the neighbors for miles in every direction that Buster was his pet seal; they wouldn't hurt him. But there was always the danger of his being shot by a stray hunter or fisherman.

Nothing bad had happened. And Buster had learned to tell time, though no one knew how he did it. Mom said he might be out in the water half a mile away from the house at ten minutes to four—and at four o'clock, when Clint was due home, he would be rocking up the front steps.

Buster had never disappointed Clint, but in these days of autumn rains the boy had to disappoint the seal. At each home-coming Buster could coax and coax Clint to go swimming, and when he refused because the weather was too cold and wet, the seal would pretend to fall over dead with disappointment. While he lay there Clint pounced on him, and they wrestled until the dogs came barking and joined in the tussle.

Usually Mom came out and told them to stop the racket. Once, when she didn't, Clint and Buster fell off the edge of the front porch and Clint rolled all the way down the steps.

Buster wasn't around the back of the house this afternoon. Probably he had been in swimming and was rocking his way up the front steps as Clint hung his dripping slicker on one of the hooks on the back porch. He opened the door and stepped into the warm kitchen, full of good smells.

Mom, who knew the time as well as Buster, was taking a big pan out of the oven.

"Just in time, Clint! I made coffee cake. You can have some if it won't spoil your appetite for supper."

"It won't, Mom. How's everything?"

"Just a quiet rainy day. Your dad went to town this morning; he'll be back for supper. There's a letter from Aunt Harriet you must see—"

"How's Buster?"

"He was out swimming. He's probably waiting for you; he always is."

As Clint opened the front door Wolf and Jerry scrambled to their feet in the shelter of the porch, wagging and barking their welcome.

Buster was nowhere in sight.

"Here, Buster! Here, Buster!"

There was no answer.

Clint looked up and down the Canal, but there was no smooth seal head pointed toward home.

Mom came out on the porch.

"Isn't he here, Clint? His clock must have been slow for once. Come in where it's warm, and have your cake. Buster's sure to be back by the time you're done."

His appetite was spoiled before he started. He ate one piece of coffee cake, then went back to the porch. As far as he could see, the gray rainy water was unbroken. He scowled at it, thinking of the time he had waited on Toandos for Buster's mother to come home. . . .

After a while Mom came out again.

"Worrying won't bring him any faster, Clint—and there's something in Aunt Harriet's letter about you. It could be important."

He might have known he would have bad

luck when there was a letter from Aunt Harriet. She had tried to talk him out of having a seal for a pet—and now Buster was missing!

In the kitchen Mom unfolded a letter.

"Harriet sent this in her letter. It's from Professor Wills at the University. He's in the department that studies the ocean."

DEAR MISS HALL:

Thank you for letting me see Clint Barlow's excellent paper on the geoduck. Several of his observations are original and, quite possibly, scientifically sound. Of at least equal interest to me is the imagination shown in the paper. As you know, Oceanography is a new science, pioneering in the last great unexplored region of the world— the ocean. And one of the first requirements for this field is the kind of scientific imagination Clint shows. Tell him from me to keep up his good work; also that *I* hope someday to have him as one of my students. Meanwhile, if Clint is ever in Seattle, I should like to show him through our laboratory. I feel sure he would see things there that would open new horizons for him.

Sincerely,

HERBERT WILLS

"Gee!" Clint said. Then he remembered about Buster, and nothing seemed good any more.

"Isn't that wonderful?" Mom said. "And you only in junior high!"

"I guess so. Yes." He stared at the letter without seeing it. "Where did Aunt Harriet get my paper?"

Mom hesitated. "She saw it when she was here last time, and borrowed it. She was going to ask you—"

"It's all right," Clint said. "I wish I knew where Buster is."

There still wasn't any sign of him; Dad wasn't home, and there were the chores to do. Clint took one more look at the darkening water, and went for his slicker and boots.

When he was milking he thought of the letter again. Dr. Wills had written about "pioneering in the last great unexplored region of the world—the ocean." That was what Clint had wanted to do, only he hadn't been able to put it in words. And Dr. Wills was going to show him the laboratory where they studied the ocean. Imagine Aunt Harriet making something like that happen! She was always meddling; trying to take him away from what he wanted to do. No, she had brought him nearer. She couldn't do both. Somewhere in his mind he thought the letter was the biggest thing that had ever happened to him. But it had come at the wrong time, when he was too worried for anything but Buster to seem important.

It was dark when Clint heard the truck, and saw the shine of headlights in the pouring rain. For the minute it seemed to him that his father could find Buster at once and make everything all right. Actually he couldn't do any more about it than Clint. But he could make things seem better.

"There's no use fretting, boy," he said in the shelter of the porch. "If he isn't back soon it's because he's found other seals, as he was intended to. You did a good job of raising him, and he's on his own now."

It sounded all right then, but at supper Clint couldn't eat much. He knew the seal better than anyone else; and Buster would have been there to meet him if he hadn't been shot, or trapped somewhere. If he knew that Buster was dead he would have to take it, and go on from there. But he felt hollow and sick when he thought of his friend suffering somewhere with no one to help him. Buster had so much good will toward everybody; he wouldn't understand Clint's not coming to help him when he was in trouble.

While Mom and Dad were eating Clint thought how wonderful it would be if there were a sound outside and Buster's funny seal face looked in the window while he tapped on the glass with a flipper. But supper ended without any sound outside except the wind and rain.

As soon as Clint could get away he put on his slicker and boots, and got his flashlight. As he was going out his father spoke to him.

"You won't be out long, will you, boy?"

"I was just going to look around the beach, Dad."

Mom said, "You shouldn't be out at all on such a night."

At the landing he shone the flashlight up and down the beach; it didn't light up anything but rain beating on wet sand; and when he swept the water with it the choppy waves broke up the light.

"Here, Buster! Here, Buster! Buster!"

When he didn't get any answer, Clint launched the little skiff, and clawed off the beach with the oars. He wasn't coming back until he found Buster. The water was rougher than he expected, and the skiff pounded and jumped as he rowed upwind.

"Here, Buster! Here, Buster!"

Every few minutes he steadied the boat with both oars in one hand while he swept the water with his flashlight. If Buster was within range his eyes would reflect the light. But there was no answering shine of eyes.

"*Here, Buster! Here, Buster!*"

In the distance, down-wind, Clint heard his father shout. He didn't answer because he didn't want to come home without his friend. The skiff was pounding heavily and throwing spray, but he was all right while he kept headed up into the wind.

After a while he heard the far-off sound of a boat being launched.

"I'm all right, Dad!" he yelled. "Don't come after me!" Probably his father couldn't hear him. Clint held the boat steady while he flashed his light over the short steep waves.

"*Here, Buster! Here, Buster!*"

He was rowing again when he heard the rumble of the outboard motor. Why couldn't Dad leave him alone?

A light flashed astern, and his father's voice shouted above the sound of the motor.

"Clint, show your light!"

He flashed the light on, shouting.

"I'm all right, Dad! Don't come after me!"

His father brought the big boat abreast of him, a dozen feet away, and throttled down the motor.

"Come back, boy! It's too rough for that little skiff, and we're in four hundred feet of water. You wouldn't stand a chance if you capsized!"

Clint was almost crying.

"I'm all right, Dad! I've got to find Buster—"

"Listen!"

The boy had already heard the giant breathing sound. It came again, louder and deeper; great calm breath after breath that filled the night as it bore down on them. Over his shoulder he saw a long blaze of phosphorescent fire leap toward his father's boat.

"Dad, look out!"

His yell was lost in a giant breathing sound and a rush of water. Out of the cold fire there heaved a great gleaming back with a fin that rose like a sickle against the sky above Dad's head. The back swerved a little at the last second, rolling forward as it swept past the boat and submerging until there was only a six-foot fin tearing through the water, shining with sparks of phosphorus.

"Killer whale!"

Clint heard his own shout, like a whisper; then his father's voice that seemed to come from a long way off.

"Look out, boy!"

He looked over his shoulder and saw the

black water boil into fire as the next killer rolled to the surface, directly ahead of his boat. It was too close and coming too fast for him to move; he could only wait for the crash. The back swerved and rushed by his tossing skiff, with a great sickle fin high above his head, dripping fire. The night was still full of vast breathing sounds and the roar of water. Over his shoulder Clint saw more of the killers, like a string of cars lit with phosphorus and carrying snoring giants. One after another, close together, they roared out of the darkness, swerved a little at the last moment, and went rolling by, some on one side of the boats and some on the other. The big solid backs and fins, glittering with sparks of phosphorus, seemed blacker than anything Clint had ever seen.

Nine of the killer whales had passed and the boats were still afloat. Clint saw his father's light flash on and heard his faint yell,

"Look out, boy! This is it!"

The flashlight shone on a great back and fin rolling up too close for any turning aside. It rushed down on them until it seemed to Clint that he could have touched it with an oar—then it submerged swiftly, with only a great fin ripping through the

water between the two boats. The skiff
tipped crazily in the fierce surge of power
rolling under it, and shipped water. It
righted itself; and Clint heard the rain rattling on his slicker, the rush of waves, the
slow, oily pulse of the outboard motor; then
his father's voice:

"Was that close enough for you, boy?
Come alongside and get in before you
swamp!"

On the way home, above the sound of
the motor, they could hear the vast breathing of the killer whales in the distance.

"I could have hung my hat on any one
of their fins," Dad said. "I never want to be
that close to blackfish again—but I wouldn't
have missed it! Did you see the phosphorus
on them? They were lit up like Christmas
trees!"

Clint knew that in daylight killer whales
liked to see how close they could come to
boats without hitting them. He had never
heard of one making a mistake. But he
didn't think these had sensed the boats in
the dark until they were almost on top of
them. Clint had been there because he
wanted to be; but Dad had only come out
to help him—and he could have lost his life.
That took the fight out of the boy.

When they had hauled the boats to

safety, Clint's father said, "Let's not say anything to your mother about that close shave. She'll be worried enough as it is."

"That's right, Dad."

In his room, trying to do his homework, Clint still saw the killer whales charging by in the dark, blacker than night and shining with sparks of phosphorus. It had been the biggest adventure of his life; but he couldn't enjoy it when he thought of Buster away somewhere in the dark, dead or trapped . . . and Clint working on Social Studies!

He remembered with sudden dread that killer whales came into Puget Sound *after* *seals.* They might have got Buster hours ago! If they hadn't yet, he could only hope that they would miss him; the Canal was so wide, and Buster so small. . . .

8. THE CASUALTY

THE angry buzz of the alarm woke Clint in the dark. He looked at the illuminated face of the clock as he turned it off—6:30, and time to get up and dress. He stumbled out of bed and discovered that he was already dressed. Buster! Buster was lost, and he had turned in with his clothes on, planning to go out later to see if the seal had come home. Instead, he had slept through. Buster would be back now, if he ever was coming.

Clint opened his window wide on the still, fresh world after the storm. The water was beginning to glimmer through mist, but the land was dark, and there wasn't any sound except the crowing of Senator, the old rooster.

He put on his shoes and ran downstairs, and out on the porch. Buster was nowhere in sight; but the dogs came around the corner of the house, shaking themselves and limbering up for a romp.

"Good dogs," Clint said. "Where's Buster?"

They didn't know.

"Let's find him."

The dogs followed him to the beach, where they ran up and down, searching. Clint thought they were doing it out of politeness, without knowing what they were looking for. And there was nothing to find.

At breakfast Clint argued that he should stay home from school and look for Buster in daylight.

"You'll do nothing of the kind," Mom said. "Your school is more important than any seal."

Dad sided with Mom. "It wouldn't do any good, boy. If Buster's in shape to get home, he will. Eat your breakfast and get off to school. You're not helping anybody by not making the best of things."

Clint argued while he tried to eat. "Buster might be caught where he needed just a little help—"

"You can't help him," Mom said. "And you're going to school. That's final!"

"Your mother's right, boy. There are a hundred and fifty square miles of Canal. You couldn't search it all in a month."

"If I don't find him in one day, I promise—" Clint heard Wolf run up on the porch, barking.

"Sounds as if your seal had come home under his own power," Dad said.

Clint was on his feet, and his father followed him out to the porch. Wolf was there alone, barking, "Come with me!" He ran down the steps ahead of them and toward the beach, where Jerry was sounding off excitedly.

From the edge of the bulkhead Clint saw the home-coming procession: Buster toiling up the beach, inch by inch, with Jerry beside him, barking encouragement, and Wolf running back and forth between the animals and the men as if he were trying to weave them together.

"Buster's hurt," Dad said.

Clint didn't have to be told. But he didn't

know how badly the seal was hurt until he was kneeling beside him on the beach. There was blood from a long gash on the head that Buster bobbed in greeting; and while he tried to raise himself on one flipper, the other hung limp and bloody. But his wounds hadn't damaged his spirit. In his greeting there was only pride because he had made his way home.

"He's been shot," Dad said. "I'm sorry, boy. It's what you had to expect."

"He's safe, now," Clint said. "He'll be all right. Won't you, Buster?"

Buster was sure he would.

"I'm afraid not," Dad said. "He might get over that scalp wound, but he'd be a cripple on land with only one front flipper."

Clint took Buster in his arms, carefully so as not to touch his wounded flipper. "I'll take him up to the house."

"All right. Then get started for school. I'll do the rest."

Clint staggered under Buster's weight, with his teeth set.

"You're not going to shoot him!"

"We don't want him to suffer any longer than he has to."

"You're not going to shoot him!" Clint repeated.

Mom met the procession at the foot of the bulkhead steps.

"Poor Buster!" There were tears in her eyes as she looked at him. "You'll have to put him out of his misery, Jim."

Clint didn't say anything until he had put Buster down on the porch, with a newspaper under his broken flipper. He hadn't realized how much the seal had grown.

"You—can't—shoot—Buster!" Clint was panting from the exertion of carrying his pet. "He's my friend! He came home because he believed in us. It took him all night, but he got here. Now he's going to have his chance—please!"

He had been talking to his parents as if they were his enemies. When he stopped, and looked at them, he knew they were his friends even if they didn't see things the way he did.

Dad cleared his throat before he spoke.

"You don't understand, boy. I want Buster to live—if he can have a good time. But he'll be a cripple with a broken flipper, even if he doesn't get infected."

"We'll set it," Clint said.

Mom looked at Dad. "What do you think?"

"I don't see how. We could maybe set the bone and put on splints. But the first time he tried to use that flipper he'd undo our work."

Clint had been thinking of that. "We'll strap the flipper to his side so he can't use it until it knits."

His father considered. "There's that bullet hole to think about. You can't treat it once the splints are on."

The boy looked at the wounded flipper. "It's still bleeding some. That'll keep the wound clean until the blood clots."

Mom agreed. "Blood is the best dressing for a wound."

"We'll take a chance," Dad said. "First we'll have to tailor some splints for that flipper; it'll need careful fitting. And we'll have to be careful not to infect the wound."

"We can measure the splints to fit the good flipper," Clint said; "they're both the same."

Dad chuckled. "I might have thought of that. Let's go to the shop and see what we can find."

They decided on some thin boatbuilding plywood that could be sterilized by boiling. At one edge the splints were nailed to a strip of wood the thickness of Buster's flipper. There was a second strip to be nailed in after the splints were in place.

At Mom's suggestion they bored two

holes in the splints. That way the dressings could be changed while the splints were on.

It seemed to Clint that those were the best hours he had ever lived. It was a school morning when no one spoke of school; he and his parents worked together, planning and inventing so Buster could have his chance. He hadn't realized what good ideas his parents had, or how much they really cared about Buster.

At ten by the kitchen clock everything was ready for the bonesetting. The room was full of disinfectant smell and steam. On one side of the table Clint stood with his arm about Buster's neck, talking to him. The radio was on; Clint was sure that music would help quiet Buster.

On the other side of the table Mom washed the broken flipper with Lysol solution. Dad lifted the boxlike splints out of the boiling water with the kitchen tongs, and Mom padded them with rolls of sterile cloth.

"All right," Dad said to Clint. "I'm counting on you not to let Buster bite anyone."

"He won't. Will you, Buster?"

The seal raised his head with a look that said he wouldn't hurt anyone in the world.

"Here we go."

Dad pulled the broken flipper out

straight. Buster winced and whimpered and looked at Clint.

"It's all right, fellow!"

"Put the splint on," Dad told Mom.

Mom fitted it snugly over the stretched flipper, and tucked more padding into the open side.

"Now the other strip of wood."

Mom put it in place; Buster whimpered and shook with quivers while she pressed it in tightly.

"Take it easy," Clint soothed him.

"You'll have to start the nails, Mary," Dad said. "I can't let go of this flipper."

Clint had never seen a woman who was any good at driving nails, but Mom managed to get them started; then Dad took the hammer with his free hand.

"Keep a good hold on him, Clint. The jarring's going to hurt."

Clint hugged the seal to him firmly.

"Steady, Buster."

Dad drove the nails skillfully. Clint was proud of the way he did it, with so little jarring.

"It's all right, Buster. Almost over now." The seal was beginning to struggle. "It's almost—" The last nail went home. "It *is* over!"

Dad let go the flipper. "That's that!"

"I feel weak," Mom said.

Everyone felt weak, except Buster, who started to raise himself on both flippers.

Clint caught the splinted flipper and held it to Buster's side.

"Not yet!"

"It's a compliment," Dad said. "He thinks we've made him as good as new!"

The flipper was strapped down to Buster's side. There was still the scalp wound to treat. Clint wanted to do the sewing up, but his father had other ideas.

"No, boy. You're the only one who can keep him from biting, and you'll need two hands to do that—maybe three."

Clint kept one arm around Buster's neck and stroked his nose while Dad shaved the hair from around the wound.

Buster winced when Mom sponged the wound; and he whimpered when she drew the edges together with a needle and white thread that had been boiled in a saucepan. There were five stitches, each one straight across and tied separately. They made the top of Buster's head look like a football with lacing.

"That's all we can do for him," Dad said, and he began helping Mom clear up the kitchen. "Have you thought where to keep him while he's laid up?"

Clint hesitated while he stroked Buster.

"I could put him in my room; it's quiet there."

"No," Mom said. "The idea! There isn't going to be any seal upstairs!"

Clint thought again.

"How about the back porch? It's quieter there than in the front."

"If you keep it neat," Mom agreed. "And give Buster's box a good scrubbing with Lysol solution."

"O. K., Mom. And I'll bore holes in the bottom so I can give him baths with the hose."

"Put the box up on two-by-fours for drainage," Dad suggested. "If you can keep him quiet and clean, he might have a chance."

Buster was installed in his hospital box on the back porch. It was quiet, and there was no view of the Canal where the seal had come to grief. But maybe he didn't like that. He looked up with friendly eyes, but he wouldn't touch the fish that Clint brought him.

"You've got to eat, Buster. You lost a lot of blood and you have to eat to get strong again."

Buster wasn't interested. He ate nothing all day. He wouldn't even touch the bottle of milk that Clint warmed for him. But in the evening, when Clint brought him milk warm from the cow, he took it almost eagerly. It seemed a good sign.

Late that night, when his parents were asleep, Clint slipped downstairs to the porch to make sure his friend was all right. Buster was moving restlessly and whimpering. The whimpering stopped when Clint petted him and talked to him. But his nose was warm when it should have been cold, as if he had a fever. He wouldn't eat or take any more milk, and when Clint started to leave the whimpering began again.

"All right, Buster! If it makes you feel better, I'll stay here awhile."

Clint was cold in his pajamas and old bathrobe, so he took his slicker from where it hung on the wall, put it on, and settled down beside the box, tucking his feet under his robe for warmth.

"I'm here, Buster. Now go to sleep."

The whimpering stopped, but began again when Clint took his hand from Buster's shoulder. It was nearly two o'clock when he was able to slip away and go upstairs to bed.

In the morning Buster took more milk fresh from the cow, and he ate a piece of salmon which Clint boned for him. His nose was still warm, but he showed more life. When Clint stopped beside him on his reluctant way to the bus, the seal managed to raise his head while he coaxed the boy to give up the ridiculous idea of going to school.

"It's only for today," Clint told him. "I'll have all day tomorrow and Sunday to look after you. I think you're going to make it, Buster!"

9. THE ROCK

BUSTER made it, with the help of penicillin and advice which Clint coaxed from Dr. Jones at Crossroads.

The young doctor said he wasn't a veterinarian—but all warm-blooded animals had a lot in common, and Clint was welcome to whatever suggestions he could make.

It was Clint who suggested bathing Buster with salt water from the Canal.

"A good idea," the doctor said. "It's what he's used to. And sea water has healing qualities that are still being discovered."

Dr. Jones didn't come to the house to treat the seal, but he did come when Mom had the grippe early in Christmas vacation —and he couldn't help seeing Buster. There was snow on the ground. The seal had grown restless and he often wriggled out of his hospital box and got about with his one good flipper.

Clint was in front of the house when the doctor was leaving. He was short and plump, with a smooth face; and he was very serious, as if he were afraid people might think him too young to be a good doctor.

"Your mother will be all right in a few days if she rests," he told Clint. "She has the mild form of influenza that's been going round."

"We'll see that Mom rests."

The doctor looked at Buster on the sled; he was prancing his head, asking Clint to haul him around some more.

"So this is your patient, Clint. Some of mine don't look as healthy." He examined the homemade splint on the flipper that was strapped to Buster's side. "Very neat. How long has it been on?"

"Nearly five weeks."

"That's quite a while. There is danger of the joint getting permanently stiff if the limb is strapped in one position too long."

"I take the straps off for a while every day," the boy explained. "I massage the joint, too."

"That's good. You've been doing the right thing." The doctor seemed to forget that he had told Clint to do it. He examined the scar on Buster's head.

"Very neat stitches."

The gash had healed, and the new hair was coming in white. It looked like a chalk mark on Buster's sleek gray head.

"Some women in the city fix their hair that way," the doctor said: "one lock of light hair among the dark; it's fashionable." He went back to examining the splint.

"How much longer do you think it should stay on?" Clint asked.

The doctor looked at him gravely. "If he were my patient, I'd take it off now."

"Now?" Suddenly it was like Christmas: the young doctor's words, and Buster on the sled in the snow, like a Christmas present that had just arrived. "You mean he's O.K.?"

"I can't promise that, Clint. The bone may not have knit for several reasons; but if it hasn't by now, it won't."

"I'll take it off now." If anything was

wrong, Clint wanted to find it out while the doctor was there.

He brought a chisel and pried up the top splint, and gently freed the flipper. Buster immediately raised himself on it.

"Don't, Buster!"

"Let him try it." The doctor bent down to examine the flipper. "Is this where it was broken?"

Clint nodded.

"It's knitted stronger than ever."

Clint hugged the seal. "Do you hear that, Buster? You're all right!"

The doctor sat on his heels in front of the sled where he could see both flippers. "They're practically alike." He got up, brushing snow from his coat. "I must be on my way."

"Gee, I don't know how to thank you! Can I let Buster swim right away?"

"It's the best possible exercise for him," the doctor said.

"Come on, Buster—swim!"

The seal pranced on his front flippers to say that he wanted to but couldn't. Then he found he was free, and floundered off the sled into the snow.

They headed for the beach, with Buster walloping along beside the boy and making seal noises that said:

"This is a good day and we're off for a swim. Let's hurry while the water is still there!"

Clint helped him down the snowy bulk-head steps and went with him as far as the water. Buster slid in at once, but turned back when he realized that the boy had stayed on the shore.

"I'm not going in, if that's what you mean. B-r-r-r! I'd freeze!"

Buster as good as told him he was being ridiculous; and when the boy still refused, he sat up in the water on his hind flipper, and coaxed and coaxed.

Clint shook his head. "No more!" He showed his empty hands.

Buster gave his silly look of despair and fell over backwards in the water, as if he had died of the shock. Then, with a power-ful lunge, he was gone. Clint had a glimpse of his mottled form flickering away under the water. He came up fifty yards off-shore, raising himself out of the water as far as his shoulders to look back at the ridiculous boy who didn't know that swimming was good in winter. He disappeared again; Clint didn't see anything of him until he popped up out of the shallow water, and rocked to the beach.

Clint patted him and laughed.

"You're out of my class, Buster; but don't forget, I taught you to swim!"

After that the seal was in the water whenever he could coax the boy to go with him to the beach; and sometimes when Clint was busy, Buster went on expeditions of his own. Twice he was gone all afternoon.

Clint never felt easy when the seal was away long; but he reminded himself how disgusted he was when Mom worried about him. And Buster was safer in winter, with no fishermen or hunters to take shots at him.

The last Saturday of vacation was stormy. Buster went to the beach alone and stayed away longer than usual. When the family sat down to supper he hadn't returned. It was the first time since he had been wounded that he hadn't been home by dark—and there was always the chance of something happening to him. Clint pretended that he only looked out of the window to see the light on the blowing sleet, but he must have looked worried.

"It's the call of the wild," Dad said over his roast pork and sweet potatoes. "Buster's growing up, boy, and so are you. If he doesn't grow into a seal and you into a man, something will be wrong. Seals weren't meant to come home to houses at night."

Clint wanted Buster to come home. And he didn't want to grow up; not yet, anyway. Vacation and being at home with his parents was nice and safe, the way it used to be before he ever went to school, when he thought it would always be that way. Right now he didn't want to grow up. At the same time he wanted it to be summer, before anything else happened to Buster. He wanted it to be summer, so they could explore the water for days at a time. . . .

Mom was asking him a question, probably for the second time.

"Clint, have you written to Aunt Harriet?"

"Not yet, Mom," he mumbled. "I'm going to."

She went on, "The day after tomorrow you go back to school. You'll have less time than ever for writing—and Harriet got Doctor Wills interested in your work—"

"I'll write the letter this evening," Clint promised.

There was a sound on the porch, and he looked up in time to see Buster's funny face rise at the window. Clint returned his happy look.

"More pork and sweet potatoes, boy?"

"I think I will, thanks."

His father smiled as he served him.

The meal that had started anxiously became a special occasion. Clint liked roast
pork and sweet potatoes; and now he was
hungry. Now everything was right; the
storm outside, and the warm kitchen and
the good food. And they were all together:
Dad, smiling his slow smile, at the head of
the table; Mom, across from Clint, looking
well again, and no longer talking about that
letter to Aunt Harriet. And at the far end
of the table, just outside the window, Buster
was like a fourth member of the family.
Sleet gleamed in the darkness behind him
and the porch was wet from the storm; but
weather meant nothing to him and he was
as comfortable as the others, in the bright
kitchen.

The holiday feeling lasted, unbroken, to
the end of vacation. Dad's logging camp
was down because of the weather, and they
had late breakfast that still allowed Clint
time to meet the school bus.

Mom was bringing more hot corn bread
from the oven when Clint saw Joe Horton's
skiff coming up from the south, close inshore.

"Joe's sure going to town early."

But instead of continuing north the big

skiff swung in to Barlow's Landing. Clint watched the old man shut off the motor, then tilt it as the boat came in to the beach.

Dad called, "Put on an extra plate, Mary, we're having company!"

When Joe was at the table he would only take a cup of coffee which he sipped politely while he talked about the weather. Finally he came to the point, with his deep-set old eyes looking embarrassed.

"Funniest thing about my cow lately. Mostly she's a good milker, but twice she didn't give any, as if she'd dried up overnight."

Clint's heart sank, and he caught a glimpse of his father's worried frown.

"Last evening in the storm," Joe said, "I went to the barn, and there was the darn'd-est thing ever; I couldn't believe my lantern at first. That seal of Clint's was under the cow, going at it like a hungry calf!"

"Gee, I'm sorry," Clint mumbled.

"It was kind of cute of him," Joe said; "only I wouldn't want him to make a habit of it."

"I should think not!" Mom said. "Before you go I'll fix you a jug of milk. We have plenty, thank goodness; but that doesn't make it up to you."

Joe looked more embarrassed. "I didn't

come to complain. I wouldn't have said anything, only I thought you'd like to know."

"That's right," Dad said. "We won't let it happen again."

Clint got up from the table. "I'll shut him up, or something, before I go to school."

Dad said, "Never mind, boy. I'll look after him. We'll see what we can plan when you come home from school."

"And hurry," Mom said. "You've just time to get to the bus."

"Don't worry about your seal," Joe said. "He's a cute thing, and he's done me no hurt."

Everyone was so kind, Clint thought, as he went up the hill. But the wonderful holidays had ended with a jolt. Dad's and Mom's and Joe's kindness was like moss on a rock. It was soft and friendly, but under it there was the hard fact that Buster had begun to get into trouble—which could wreck everything.

10. A TOUGH DECISION

THE shop was in one end of the woodshed, and while Clint worked at the
bench he talked to Buster.

"Sure it's Saturday; but if we're not outdoors, whose fault do you think it is?"

Buster didn't know anything about faults;
he coaxed to go swimming.

"You had a swim this morning," Clint reminded him; "and you'll have another pretty
soon. But what about school days? You
don't want to be locked in the woodshed
five days a week, do you?"

Buster thought it over while Clint put another rivet in the harness he was making, held it on the vise, and hammered the rivet flat. Then he barked again.

"We gave you your chance after Christmas vacation. And what did you do?"

Urrgh! urrgh!

"I'll tell you what you did. You went to the pasture and milked Juno. Then you went to the harbor and stole a big salmon that Karl Larson had caught for himself. Was that nice?"

Buster's head bobbed at the sound of salmon.

"He shot at you, too! You might have been killed!"

Buster had no answer for that.

"So we had to lock you in the woodshed to save your life." Clint flattened another rivet and looked at the brass-studded collar hanging on a nail above the bench.

"I spent my own money on a fine collar for you, so you could be on a leash outside when I was away. And what did you do?"

The seal didn't remember.

"You slipped out of the collar the first time my back was turned—that's what you did. With that streamlined neck of yours you shed a collar the way you shed water."

114

At the mention of water Buster pranced and tried to coax Clint toward the door; but the boy went on.

"After you were hurt you were good for a long time, with your flippers strapped down. This harness will let you use your flippers—so don't think up ways of getting out of it. If you keep it on, you can be outdoors all day."

Urrgh! urrgh! Buster wanted to be out that minute.

"You just be patient and I'll be done in time for you to have a swim before lunch."

But the harness wasn't quite finished when Dad came to say that lunch was ready.

Dad examined the harness approvingly. "Strong enough to hold a bull." He waited while Clint set the remaining rivets.

"There." Clint put down the hammer. "Come on, Buster, you can try it out while we're eating."

Buster willingly followed them to the back yard; less willingly he let them pass the harness under him and buckle the straps at his back.

"Make them tight," Dad advised. "If he wriggles out of this once, it'll be harder to hold him next time."

Clint thought the straps were too tight— but he could loosen them afterward. Almost anything was better than having Buster get away and into trouble.

One end of the leash was on a ring on the clothesline; Clint snapped the other end to the ring at the back of the harness.

"There you are, Buster! You can go up and down the yard like a trolley bus. Be good, and I'll take you for a swim right after lunch."

"I believe that'll hold him," Dad said. "Now let's skedaddle before your mother comes after us."

Mom was already coming; she called to them from the back porch.

"Lunch is on and it's getting cold. I don't know which of you boys is the worst!"

"We just finished a real job," Clint told her. "Buster can be outdoors all day now without getting into trouble."

Dad was in good spirits when they sat down to eat.

"Once a job like that is done, it's done!" he said. "We can forget it and go on to other things."

Clint felt the same way until about the middle of the meal when he heard a dragging sound on the porch, followed by scuffling and scratching just outside the window; then Buster's cheerful whiskered

116

face appeared at the pane, his flippers holding onto the sill.

"Slipped out of his harness," Dad said. "Well, new gear always needs adjusting."

Clint was already planning how the harness could be made to stay on, but he didn't say anything. Mom thought the harness had already taken too much time, and he would have to work on it another hour or two.

It took him all afternoon, with occasional help from Dad. But when they had added loops that fitted close around Buster's flippers, it seemed impossible that he could ever get out of the harness without help.

In the morning the harness was still on, and Buster was sulking in the corner of the back steps. Clint hugged him and released him for a swim.

"I know you don't like this rig, fellow; but it'll save your life. I'm going to give you a tub of water in the yard so you can dunk yourself while I'm at school."

The real test of the harness came on Monday, when Clint was gone all day. It held. In the days that followed the boy worried less. But his conscience never felt right when he came out of the orchard and saw Buster sitting up in the galvanized tub in the back yard like a sentry, watching for his friend to come and set him free for a few hours. Seals were meant to be free all their lives.

On Friday afternoon Clint was feeling better about things as he came down the hill from the school bus. Ahead of him were two days with Buster; and it was only nine weeks to the end of school. Nine weeks till summer, when the two of them would be free to swim and sail and explore. . . . That is, if nothing bad happened before then.

From the edge of the orchard Clint saw the galvanized tub and the leash hanging from the overhead wire near the woodshed. But he couldn't see Buster. Maybe he was inside the shed, though it wasn't like him to be anywhere but sitting up in the tub— unless he had tangled his leash on something in the shed and choked himself.

Clint ran the last fifty yards and entered the shed with a rush. He looked wonderingly at the empty harness on the end of the leash. Every strap was buckled as it should be, but Buster had slipped out of it like a Houdini. And he was nowhere in sight.

In the house his mother was talking on the telephone; she was being extra polite, as if it were someone she didn't know very well, asking her to call next time she was passing, and promising to do the same when *she* was down that way.

Clint waited for his mother to hang up.

"Buster's off again, Mom. Slipped out of his harness."

Mom sighed. "As if I didn't know! It must have happened this morning when I was busy with the housecleaning. First I knew of it was when I had a call from Mr. Ross, up near town. He had just chased Buster out of the pasture because he was milking one of the cows. And that was Mrs. Beyer I was talking to just now. I've never even seen her."

"They live in the new house south of the harbor," Clint told her. "They're city people. What did she want?"

"She's scared out of her wits. She was in her living room playing records when she saw a 'sea monster' outside the window, holding onto the window sill and swaying in time to the music."

"Is he there now, Mom?"

"No, she kept the player going while she called the game warden, and someone in the office told her we had a pet seal. So she called here, but by that time the player had stopped and Buster was gone."

It was the biggest fuss that had been

made about Buster—just because he loved
music and had time to enjoy it!

"I'll go look for him," Clint said. "This
time I'll see that he doesn't get away."

He didn't have to look for Buster. When
he got to the beach the seal's head popped
up fifty yards from the landing. He rose
until his shoulders were out of water and
made frisky motions with his head, telling
Clint to come on in. Then he dived, to
reappear in the shallow water almost at
Clint's feet. He came out, frisking and beam-
ing good will; Clint couldn't even scold him
for having made so much trouble.

Buster followed him around faithfully
while he did the chores. But at milking
time Clint locked him in the woodshed;
Buster knew too much about cows.

Dad laughed over Buster's latest adventure. Then he said seriously:

"Remember, Clint, you were only to keep
the seal as long as he stayed out of mischief."

Clint was close to panic.

"He hasn't done any real harm, Dad. And
I'll tie him up so he can't get away again,
ever. Please—"

Dad looked unhappy.

"I suppose you could fasten him with
chains, or build a jail for him so there

wouldn't be a chance of his breaking loose and having fun."

The boy choked back a guilty feeling.

"Buster has fun when I'm home, Dad. And it's only nine weeks to the end of school—"

Dad didn't say anything more until the next afternoon when he came home from the booming ground at the harbor. Clint and Buster were at the landing, playing one-way catch. They had been fishing, and the seal was sitting up in the water catching pieces of flounder the boy threw to him. Dad nosed his boat up on the beach and sat in the bow watching.

Clint was tossing from thirty feet away and Buster, with his snaky neck and perfect sense of timing, never missed a catch. He scrounged down for low ones, reached to one side or the other, and stretched up for the high ones, always as if the pieces of fish were coming to him in slow motion and he couldn't miss if he tried.

"You could sell him to the Yankees for an outfielder," Dad called. "I couldn't do any better myself."

"Bet you can't do as well," Clint challenged, hurling the last piece of fish in the direction of the boat.

There was a glint of steel as Dad raised one foot; the fish smacked against the sole

of the shoe and stuck there on the sharp
calks.

"How's that?"

"At least you can't do any better."

"The heck I can't! Can Buster catch with
his foot?"

They argued the point for a while, then
Dad looked serious.

"Come over and sit down, boy."

Clint sat on the gunwale near his father,
and after a minute Buster came out of the
water and lay near Clint's feet.

Dad's blue eyes looked at the boy, friendly and questioning and a little sorry.

"Are you smart, Clint?"

"Not very."

His father smiled.

"Then you're like the rest of us. But you
can try to be smart."

Clint smiled in return, but he was uneasy.

"How smart, Dad?"

"Smart enough to do what you know you
have to do, instead of waiting till you're
kicked into doing it."

"Like what, Dad?"

His father answered slowly. "Like giving
up your seal."

"No! No, Dad! Buster's my friend, and he
hasn't done any harm. What if he did milk

the Rosses' cow? I'll pay for it with my own money. And he didn't do old Mrs. Beyer any harm by listening to her records. If she doesn't know what a seal is like, it's her own fault. She doesn't have to be that ignorant. And I'll see that Buster doesn't ever get away again."

Dad stopped him with a smile.

"Take it easy, boy. I don't think Buster's done anything bad. He's just been a seal—as much as he could be. The real danger is from you."

"I've done my best," Clint told him. "I've done the best I knew—"

"Sure, Clint, you did a good job of raising him. You took care of him when he was hurt, when I didn't think he had a chance, and you got him well again. You've raised him, and there's nothing more you can do but harm him—unless you turn him loose and let him be a seal."

Clint swallowed.

"But he'd only come home, Dad. And if he were free to go as he pleased, he'd be shot in a week."

"Suppose it was a place where people didn't live—where he had a real chance?"

"The Canal isn't that kind of place," Clint argued.

"Look, boy; when I was at the Harbor, I

talked with Captain Johanson. He's leaving
for Alaska tomorrow. He could take Buster
along and turn him loose some place where
he'd be happy—where he'd have a real
chance."

Clint swallowed again.

"I don't imagine Captain Johanson would
want to be bothered taking a seal along."

"I spoke to him about it; he said he'd be
glad to."

Clint felt trapped.

"You mean it's all arranged?"

"Only if you see it that way, boy. I want
you to decide."

Clint didn't answer, so his father went on.

"There are places on the British Colum-
bia coast where I wouldn't mind being
turned loose. Like Gardner Sound. There are
three banks of islands between the Inside
Passage and the ocean; and on the land
side there are big inlets—like the spokes of
a wheel. Some of those inlets go back a hundred miles into the Canadian mountains, in
the most beautiful country you ever saw.
Nobody lives there, and on some of the inlets you wouldn't see a boat once a year."

As Clint listened he felt that by some
magic he was back in a man's world, hear-
ing about the things his father wanted to
do.

"When we build our boat and go to Alaska, we can visit Gardner Sound, can't we?" If they did that he would see Buster again.

"Sure," Dad said. "We'll spend a week there—maybe a month. It would take a whole summer to explore all the channels between the islands, and the big inlets going back into the mountains. . . ."

Clint petted the seal's friendly head as he listened. It didn't seem so bad, thinking of Buster in a wonderful new world where he and his father wanted to go—and where they would find Buster when they did go.

When they were going up to the house, with the seal walloping along beside them, Clint said:

"Dad, Captain Johanson can take Buster if he promises to turn him loose in Gardner Sound."

11. CANDLEFISH LIGHT

IT WAS about ten o'clock Sunday morning
when Clint saw the *Snow Queen* coming up from the south. She was an old-style
halibut schooner with her pilothouse aft,
and tall masts that carried riding sails
when she was fishing out to westward off
the Aleutians.

Buster wasn't going that far, but just
thinking about faraway places made Clint
feel lonely. Sitting on the front porch with
one arm around Buster, he hugged the seal
to himself.

"Dad," he called. "Dad, they're coming!"

His father came out, lighting his pipe.

"So they are."

The Canal was like glass, and the white schooner was reflected crookedly in the bow wave that bent the smooth water into rolls without breaking it. Now the fluttering cough of the Diesel engine was echoing against the shore.

"Well, Clint, let's shove off."

At the last minute Mom came out to say good-by to Buster.

"I know they'll take good care of him on the way," she said, petting him. "He'll have a good life. Won't you, Buster?"

Buster bobbed his head to say that he would always have a good life.

Mom wasn't going out to the schooner. Captain Johanson hadn't exactly forbidden it, but he had discouraged her. It is supposed to be bad luck for a woman to be on board a fishing boat that is sailing for the north. Not that the captain was superstitious, but it would make his crew nervous.

It helped a little that Buster was going away in a man's world; and Clint needed all the help there was.

On the beach he and his father tipped the little skiff and Buster floundered trustingly over the gunwale. Getting into a boat usually meant going fishing with Clint, and the seal was happy.

The *Snow Queen* was lying-to, waiting for them. Fishermen in woolen shirts were standing at the rail, and fastened to the rigging were bamboo fishing staffs with corks and pennants.

As Dad brought the skiff alongside, two fishermen caught it with boathooks, and Clint heard Captain Johanson's big, easy voice.

"So there's our passenger. He has his sea legs, I bet. You can pass him up, Jim."

Buster weighed as much as Clint, and together the boy and his father lifted the seal to the rail, where he was taken by big, hook-scarred hands.

Captain Johanson was a stocky man, past middle age, with steady gray eyes and a grave smile which seemed to promise that Buster would be well-cared-for.

"Come on board," he said. "You'll want to see the cabin we have for your passenger. And there is always time for a cup of coffee, you bet."

As Clint went over the rail with his father, he noticed the clean scrubbed deck, the nested yellow dories, and the fishing gear. Then he had eyes for nothing but the barred crate where Buster was asking to be let out. His whimpering stopped when Clint sat on the deck and reached in to stroke the sleek head.

"It's all right, Buster," Clint soothed him. "It's all right. You're going to a wonderful place—like the Canal before there were people here. We're coming up in our own boat before long, and you and I can explore around for weeks. Look out for killer whales, and don't tackle an octopus too big for you—and don't take any wooden nickels, Buster." While they visited, the fluttering sound of the exhaust went on like birds escaping. Then Dad's voice broke through.

"Time to go ashore, boy!"

Clint got up and Captain Johanson put a big hand on his arm.

"We'll take good care of him, you bet. I'll leave him deep in a fjord where there are no settlers, and no boats."

Clint looked down at the big hand resting on his arm; it was deeply scarred where it had been caught by a flying hook on halibut gear racing out into the Aleutian sea. That must have hurt, Clint thought.

Later, looking out of his upstairs window at home, Clint saw the *Snow Queen* and her white wake grow smaller in the distance and disappear behind the peninsula.

Then he picked up the notebook where he had written his observations about Buster: *What I Learned from a Pet Harbor Seal.* It seemed to him that he had forgotten to notice some of the most important things.

He was still frowning at the notebook when he heard a car come down the hill and stop near the house. He hoped whoever it was would go away—he didn't want to see anyone.

Downstairs he heard strange voices and familiar ones; one of them was Aunt Harriet's. Clint stiffened. She couldn't be blamed for what had happened to Buster; but just the same, she didn't have to come to crow about it!

"Clint," his mother called from the foot of the stairs, "we have company. Can you come down?"

He went to the landing.

"Please, Mom, I'd rather not."

His mother came upstairs, patient and smiling. She had an apron on over her best dress; she had known the company was coming.

"Clint, there's someone downstairs I'm sure you'd like to see."

"I don't want to see anyone, Mom. Who is it?"

"Doctor Wills and his wife. They came out with Harriet."

He didn't know any Doctor Wills. Then he remembered the man at the university who had read his paper on geoducks.

"Not Doctor Wills the oceanographer?"

"He's the one."

"Gee, Mom!"

"You will come down, won't you?"

"Sure I will; right away!"

Clint had pictured Professor Wills as a big, important-looking man who would know the answers to all his questions. But he was shy and gray-haired, and he asked more questions than he answered. Clint liked him, though.

"I had counted on seeing your seal," the professor said. "So many people kill seals and so few make pets of them. I almost did myself, once. Someone brought a seal to the marine station at Friday Harbor—it couldn't have been more than a week old. I wanted to take it home to study its behavior, but Myra drew the line at that. Didn't you, dear?"

Mrs. Wills was big and friendly, with gray hair and a pink face. She smiled at the professor as if he were a little boy.

"I'd draw it again, Herb! A seal!"

"You see the obstacles in the way of science, Clint!"

Clint smiled a little proudly. His parents had been more help than a scientist's wife.

"Did you keep notes on your seal?" the professor asked.

"Some."

"I'd like to see them, if I may."

"Sure, Professor Wills. I'll get them for you."

Clint started up the stairs, and the professor followed him.

"I'll come with you. I'd like to see your collection."

"I haven't a real collection; just things I picked up around here."

The professor took it all in with an appraising eye.

"Very good, Clint. Sea fans, and basket starfish shells—you have some rare ones—and sea stones. And what's this on the wire above your desk?"

"A dried candlefish—in case the electricity goes off."

Professor Wills was thrilled.

"I knew the Indians used them, and the pioneers on the coast; I've seen them alive, and dissected them. But I never got around to drying any. Do they give much light?"

"You can light that one." Clint pulled

down the shade. "I have lots more. Mom says they make my room smell; but I don't notice it except when I first come in."

The professor struck a match and touched it to the thin dried tail. There was a little sputter, then the candlefish burned with a clear bright flame.

"Wonderful! It makes a lovely light." He took Scammon's *Marine Mammals* from the shelf and opened it. "You can actually read by it!" But he was more interested in watching the burning candlefish. "What good combustion! And hardly any smell!"

Clint opened the big coffee can in which he kept his supply.

"I'll give you some to take home."

"I'd better not, Clint." Then his face brightened. "Yes, on second thought, I will. I can use them in the laboratory."

Clint rolled a handful in a piece of theme paper and the professor thrust them in his pocket.

When the candlefish burned out Clint put up the shade, and he could see again the great headland of Toandos Peninsula dividing the Canal. He had found Buster there, and there he had lost him when the *Snow Queen* disappeared behind the headland.

"And now," the professor said, "shall we look at your notes?"

Clint gave the professor his worn book.

"It looks kind of moldy—Buster tried to eat it once. I guess it had the smell of fish on it from my hands."

The professor chuckled at the sharp teeth marks.

"Right out of the seal's mouth! I know the notes are genuine."

"They're not very good," Clint told him; "and they're not all about Buster. I put in everything I thought of about warm-blooded animals and the sea."

"That should make it more interesting."

He read rapidly at first, then more slowly, pausing to talk things over, his eyes bright behind his rimless glasses.

"This is good, Clint, about the bear ancestors of the seal, who fed on spawning salmon in a creek, and followed the salmon into deeper and deeper water until at last they developed flippers and turned into seals. It could have happened that way."

"I got the idea watching bears along the creek in the fall," Clint explained. "I never saw one swim out after a salmon, but some of them seemed to be thinking about it."

"It's happening today with polar bears," the professor explained. "They spend so much time in the water that it's a question now whether they're land or sea animals.

134

They're very poorly equipped for swimming, though."

"Maybe that's why they have such bad tempers," Clint said, "doing something they're not suited for."

The professor chuckled. "I noticed you bring up that question: *Why seals, related to the surly bear, are good-natured and playful. Is it the influence of the sea?*"

He went on with the notes.

"So you had a close-up of killer whales? *Whales seem to enjoy life more than fish; maybe that's because they're warm-blooded and get the feel of the ocean better than fish do. A fish, being the same temperature as the water it is in, hardly knows the sea is there.*"

The professor went on, reading and commenting.

"So you actually saw what your seal caught in the water when he was feeding— squid, and a little octopus, and—"

They were interrupted by Aunt Harriet, who came to say that lunch was ready. She sniffed as she entered the room.

"This place smells like an Indian camp."

"We were burning a candlefish on the altar of science," Professor Wills explained. He closed the notebook and put it carefully on the table.

"Clint, I can see that you have the makings of an oceanographer!"

"Gee! Do you really mean that, Professor Wills?" It seemed to Clint that the professor was opening up an exciting new world for him.

At lunch Professor Wills said he was hungry for oysters, and Dad suggested an expedition. He got out the big skiff with the outboard motor, and they all went to Pirate Bay.

Dad built a fire near the foot of the bluff where there were drift logs to sit on. While he was building the fire, Aunt Harriet talked about Buster as if she had raised him, and she asked Clint to show them where he had found the baby seal. Clint led them to the place and showed them the spot among the boulders.

"Most interesting!" the professor said. "Shelter and concealment a few yards from the water at high tide. The mother seal couldn't have chosen a better place." He lay down among the rocks and propped himself on his elbows to get a seal's-eye view. "It's even better than I thought. For such concealment it gives a wide view of the beach and the water."

Clint took his turn lying among the rocks, getting a view of the world as Buster had first seen it: sand, and granite boulders that seemed to tower up like cliffs; the sloping beach and the wide water; and the foothills of the Olympics rising on the other shore. It looked like a fine, safe world for a seal. But it wasn't.

Afterward they filled a gunny sack with oysters and Dad announced they could have an oyster roast. Everyone was for it except Aunt Harriet, who had left her warm coat at home. So they all went home. Aunt Harriet was always doing things like that, Clint told himself.

When he was feeling maddest at his aunt he remembered that if it hadn't been for her there wouldn't have been any expedition and he might never have met Professor Wills. He didn't know what to think.

The company left at dark, carrying large sacks of oysters and promising to get together again soon. The professor promised to send Clint some books that would help him in his studies.

The excitement lasted until Clint went up to his room. There he couldn't think of anything but Buster on the *Snow Queen;* Buster wondering why Clint wasn't there and not knowing what was happening to him.

He wouldn't know until the day after to-morrow, when he would be put overboard in a great lonely inlet where there were no houses on shore, and no boats passed. Even then he wouldn't understand. Buster had so much good will for people that he would wonder why he had been left in a place where there weren't any.

12. THE FACE
AT THE WINDOW

Thursday afternoon was stormy. Clint
came home in driving rain, running from
the bus to the house because he had on his
good shoes when he should have been wear-
ing boots.

As he came out of the orchard he felt a
sharp pang at not seeing Buster sitting up
in his tub, waiting for him. Then the rain
let loose as if the clouds had burst, and he

forgot everything as he dashed for the back porch, spattering water at every leap.

Inside it was like old times: the warm kitchen and the good baking smells; his mother taking a pie out of the oven, and everything made warmer and nicer by the roar of rain over the house.

"For goodness' sake, Clint! Won't you ever learn not to trust the weather? Those shoes will never be the same again!"

"I forgot, Mom," Clint apologized. "But a little water won't hurt them. Is there any mail for me?"

"Put on your slippers first—and stuff those shoes with newspaper while they dry or they'll never have any shape." She handed him some newspaper from the pile on the back porch. "I'll get you some pie and coffee."

He moved fast and was dry-shod by the time Mom had a big piece of pie and a steaming cup of coffee on the table.

"Thanks, Mom. *Mmm.* That pie smells good!"

Beside his plate his mother had placed an air-mail letter from Ketchikan, Alaska, addressed in pencil. It was the letter he had been hoping for, but he opened it slowly because it couldn't contain any really good news.

THE FACE AT THE WINDOW

DEAR CLINT:

I write this as we are crossing Dixon Entrance.

Your seal was a good passenger and he made friends with everyone. This morning at 9:12 we set him at liberty in Gardner Sound. First we went for half an hour up a big fjord that opens from the Inside Passage. I don't know any better place for a seal to live. Or a man, if he don't mind the loneliness.

The only live things we saw on the fjord were fish jumping and eagles flying. He can use the fish, and the eagles will not bother him. He ate well on the trip and was in good health when we left him.

I send my best wishes to your father and mother.

CARL JOHANSON

Clint handed the letter to Mom, who read it briskly and handed it back.

"I knew Captain Johanson would get him there safely. Buster will have a good life, Clint, and don't you worry about him. Now I have to fix supper, and you have chores to do."

Buster had never meant a lot to Mom and it was easy for her to dust him off her life. But Clint couldn't forget so easily. The seal was the best friend he had ever had, closest to the mysteries he wanted to explore.

He went upstairs to change to his working clothes. Everything in his room reminded him of Buster, like the piece of purple seaweed on the wall above his table. They got it the time they were exploring Jackson Cove; Buster had come up with the seaweed in his mouth to show he had reached bottom in ten fathoms of water. Now there was a sort of magic about the piece of seaweed; it was the kind Clint used to see in his dreams of the underwater world—purple seaweed waving in the dim deep tide. It was a sign that Buster had understood.

On the table was a book Professor Wills had sent him—*The Sea Around Us*. At any other time Clint would have stayed up all night to finish it; but he didn't feel like reading just now. The note that had come with the book was lying beside it; Clint read the ending again before going downstairs.

> You have made a good beginning in your studies; keep it up. Call on me whenever I can be of help.
>
> > Sincerely,
> > HERBERT WILLS
>
> P.S. Here is the list of high-school subjects for majoring in oceanography.
>
> > H.W.

Dad and Mom had been more excited over the letter than Clint. Mom said he should go to a high school where he would have more advantages than at Crossroads. When his mother went on like that she sounded like Aunt Harriet. It made him feel lonely and homesick just thinking about being away. There wasn't any sense to it.

He put the note in the book and went down to do the chores. His father was just getting home and Clint followed him to the kitchen to give him Captain Johanson's letter. Dad read it thoughtfully and handed it back.

"Cheer up, boy," he said, laying his hand on Clint's shoulder. "I miss the rascal, too. But he had to be weaned. He'll grow up to be a seal, the way he was intended; and you'll grow, too."

Clint smiled at his father as he reached for the milk pail. As long as they both missed Buster he didn't mind being lonely.

At supper Dad was in such good spirits that Mom said he must have had good news.

"Not bad, anyway," he said. "Today I finished logging that forty. It's all in the water without an accident." He knocked on the table for luck, as if the logs in the boom might still find a way to hurt someone.

"And how is the market?" Mom knew the work wasn't finished when you got the logs cut and into the water; they still had to be sold.

"The price of logs is up," Dad said. "Maybe this year we can do some of the things we've talked about. We can wish, anyway."

"I wish we might build our big cruising boat," Clint said.

"I'm going to buy a new hat," Dad said.

Mom laughed. "Is that all?"

"Maybe not," Dad admitted. "But I think best with my hat on, and a new hat might give me new ideas."

"Make it a sailor hat, Dad, so you'll think about the boat."

"We could use a home freezer," Mom remembered. "If you and Clint ever get that elk you're always talking about, we'd have some place to keep it."

It was good, Clint thought, sitting at supper with Dad and Mom and making plans. It was particularly good on a stormy evening like this, with the rain enclosing the house in a wall of sound, making the room seem safe and warm. In rains like this, when Clint was small, he used to pretend there were just the three of them in the world— Mom and Dad and himself—living in a cave in the Ice Age. The rain outside couldn't

reach them in their warm cave, where they
had everything....

Clint's thoughts were interrupted by a
rattling of the window, and he turned
quickly to see what caused it.

There, looking in at the window, was a
seal's happy, whiskered face! He was knocking on the glass with one flipper.

"BUSTER!"

"Well, I'll be—" Dad set down his coffee
cup with a bang and burst out laughing.
Clint tore out of the room and out on the
porch. He could still hear Dad laughing as
he hugged warm, wet Buster, who made
joyful noises as he bobbed his head and
tried to lick Clint's face.

The porch lights were turned on and
Clint's parents came out. Dad was chuck-
ling as he patted Buster's head.

"You've set a swimming record, fellow.
The air mail beat you by only half a day!"

The dogs came bounding out of the rain
and up on the porch, barking their welcome
and shaking water over everyone. In the
uproar of the homecoming it suddenly oc-
curred to Clint that Buster must have been
swimming day and night, without stopping
to grab a bite on the way.

"Mom, can I give Buster some of the salmon in the refrigerator?"

"Of course." Mom smiled. "He must be starved!"

While Clint cut up the salmon, Mom put on a coat and they held a supper party on the porch, with Buster doing the eating. He reached to catch each piece as Clint threw it to him, wolfing it down and coaxing for more. When it was all gone, he still coaxed.

"No more!" Clint shook his head and showed the seal his empty hands.

Buster gave his silly look of despair and turned over on the porch, playing dead. Clint pounced on him and wrestled with him; the dogs barked and jumped on both boy and seal with their front feet; Mom and Dad laughed; and the rain roared down.

When at last they broke it up, Dad said, "Let's get into the house. This isn't a night for men or dogs to be out." He looked at Mom. "I'm going to let the dogs in by the fire."

"No, Jim. You men are enough trouble. Not the dogs."

"Buster's coming, too."

"No, Clint! The dogs can come in if you

must make a wreck of the place. But not Buster—not in the living room!"

Dad winked at Clint.

"We'll let the dogs in, anyway, Mary."

He opened the door, and Wolf and Jerry marched in, on their best behavior, with Buster walloping after them.

"Stop him!" Mom cried. "Don't let him come in!"

Dad let him pass.

"Too late, Mary. We'll just let him stay a little while; I want to see what he'll do."

The dogs were already lying in front of the fire. Buster rocked to the hearth, nudged Wolf with his flipper, telling him to move over, and settled down beside him. Clint settled himself beside Buster, giving him a nudge and then putting an arm around him.

Mom laughed in spite of herself.

"I declare! The livestock that collects on our hearth!"

"We're all warm-blooded," Clint told her; "and Buster has just swum a thousand miles."

"About six hundred," Dad corrected him. "At that, he must have kept going day and night without taking a wrong turn. I'd like to see the navigator who can do that without charts!"

"And after he'd been over the course only

once—in a crate where he couldn't see anything." Clint looked with admiration at Buster, who was blinking contentedly into the fire.

"It's instinct," Mom said, as if the seal didn't deserve any credit.

"I wish I had that kind of instinct," Dad said.

"I guess people did have it once," Clint suggested; "but they lost it."

Dad took his pipe from his mouth and nodded.

"Buster wouldn't need a chronometer for his navigating," Clint told his parents. "He always knew to the minute when I was getting home from school. Didn't he, Mom?"

"Right to the minute," Mom said.

"That's an instinct a few people still have," Dad said. "I worked with a logger once who could tell what time it was, day or night, without a watch. He never missed it by more than a minute or two."

Mom put down her sewing and looked at the four on the hearth.

"You men! You'd take us back to the Stone Age! We've got present problems to tackle."

"What problems, Mom?"

"The same problem we had last week. We're right back where we started with Buster—only we've got him out of the back yard into the living room. What are we going to do now?"

Clint knew what they *wouldn't* do, and he put his arm around Buster again.

"I won't give him up, Mom! He's my friend and he's here because he wants to be. If you send him away again, I'm going too!"

Mom looked at Dad, and Dad looked puzzled.

"It wouldn't do any good to send him away, Mary. If we shipped him to Australia, or Cape Horn, he'd be back in a few weeks. He seems to think we're very special people."

Clint tightened his hold on Buster.

"He remembers how we set his broken flipper, and how Mom sewed up the wound on his head—"

"Flattery won't help, Clint." Mom tried to sound sharp, but she couldn't help smiling. "You know Buster was getting to be a nuisance. He'll be worse now. We can't keep him."

"But he swam hundreds of miles to get home, Mom!" Clint pleaded. "We've got to give him a chance! I'll see that he doesn't ever get into trouble again. And there's a lot I can learn about him. Professor Wills said I made a good start and it was too bad I couldn't go on—"

Professor Wills was the strongest argument Clint could use with his mother, but she had an answer for him.

"Remember that Mrs. Wills wouldn't let even the professor keep a seal."

"That was different, Mom. They would have had to keep it in an apartment. I promise I'll look after Buster so he won't be any trouble. It's almost summer and I'll soon be out of school—"

Mom shook her head.

Dad was smiling.

"You say you can, your mother says you can't. I suppose we could give Buster another chance." Dad's eyes consulted Mom, then looked evenly at Clint. "But if he gets into trouble again, we get rid of him."

"All right," Mom nodded; "if Clint will remember that."

The boy hugged the seal tight.

"I'll remember, Mom. You'll see."

13. THE LAST STRAW

CLINT walked down the hill whistling "... into the wild blue yonder." Not because he had any desire to become a flyer; but on a day like this he felt that he could take off from the hill without a plane and zoom out, over the orchard which was white and pink with blossoms, over the sparkling blue waters of the Canal and the high woods of Toandos, and back again.

It had taken him a whole week end to dig post-holes and to stretch wire fencing for the pen in the back yard, but it was worth it. Buster had kept out of trouble ever since. Now there were only six more weeks of school left, and Clint felt he could almost hold his breath that long. Tomorrow Len and Phil Decker and the Lawson boys were coming over for a look at the seal that had made the record trip from Gardner Sound. Old Buster had learned a thing or two since the boys had tried to give him his first swimming lesson!

The wild blue yonder darkened as he came out of the orchard. There was no Buster sitting up in the tub to welcome him, and he wasn't in sight anywhere. Clint walked the last distance with feet like lead, and stared into the empty pen. The gate was latched, but the flattened grass and a few hairs on the gate and post showed where Buster had squeezed through—changing his shape the way he had when he slipped out of his harness.

It didn't seem possible, but it was a fact —Buster was gone!

Clint ran around the house and down to the beach; but the only thing in sight on the water was a distant boat moving at trolling speed. He thought of taking out one of the boats and searching for Buster, but that might do more harm than good. He might search for hours without any luck, and meanwhile the chores would not get done. That would be the last straw. Besides, there was always the chance that Buster would come home without getting into mischief.

He turned back toward the house, and his mother met him on the porch.

"He's not in sight?"

Clint shook his head.

"He got away early this afternoon," Mom said. "He was there at one, when I looked, and by two o'clock he was gone."

"It's my fault, Mom. I should have put a hook on the bottom of the gate."

"There's nothing you can do about it now," she said. "Come in and have your snack. I made some jelly doughnuts today."

But even Mom's jelly doughnuts couldn't tempt him.

"There haven't been any complaints about him," Mom smiled encouragingly. "Maybe he's behaving himself."

"I hope so, Mom." Though it wouldn't be like Buster.

Clint was still hoping when he let the cows into the barn and started to milk Juno. If he had looked at her udder first, he wouldn't have started. Buster must have gone to the pasture for a snack of milk before starting on his adventures.

When Dad came home Clint told him that Buster was gone and the cow hadn't given any milk, and he only said, "Buster has really hit his stride!"

That evening Clint studied downstairs. He started whenever the telephone jangled, but each time it was for some other family on the line. Their own signal, two long rings followed by a short one, didn't sound until almost bedtime. Dad answered it. Clint held his breath.

"Yes, this is Barlow. How are you, Sheriff?"

Mom nodded as if to say she had expected it. Clint wasn't too surprised.

"Yes," Dad said again. "We have, and he's at large. No, perfectly harmless and good-natured. He what? No! That must have been a surprise. Was he toasting marshmallows? Oh, yes, he loves music." Dad listened for a while, then asked, "What did they do?"

There was another silence at the phone, and Mom sighed over the wool sock she was darning.

"A person listening would think that someone in our family was peculiar."

Dad was speaking again.

"He did? That's too bad. We'll get them some new ones."

Clint's heart sank, and it was a struggle for him to look up when his father came back from the phone.

"That's that!" Dad said.

"What happened?" Mom asked. "What did he do this time?"

"The sheriff had a complaint from the Porters—some new people near Triton Cove. The Porters had company, and when the company was going they all went out to the car, leaving the door open. When Mrs. Porter went back to the living room, a seal was making himself at home in front of the fire, listening to the radio; she said it was dancing. Her husband thought she must be mistaken. Anyway, she screamed and ran out. Mr. Porter came and tried to drive the seal out, and Mrs. Porter came to help him. Apparently Buster thought they were playing; he wouldn't leave. In the excitement Mr. Porter backed into a table and knocked over a goldfish bowl. Buster snapped up both goldfish and took off, leaving the house in quite a state."

"Where is he now?" Mom asked.

"Who knows? But I wouldn't be surprised if we had another phone call before long."

"You can't blame Buster," Clint told them. "It's my fault for not fixing the gate better. I'll see that it doesn't happen again."

Dad shook his head.

"No, boy. I'm not blaming Buster. He's a fine seal. But he just doesn't fit in."

"He certainly doesn't," Mom agreed. "We'll have to get rid of him."

"First we'll have to catch him." Dad looked at Clint. "You made an agreement, boy, and you'll have to keep it. Buster goes as soon as we can figure out what to do with him."

There were no more phone calls that night or in the morning, and Clint felt hopeful. It might be weeks before they could decide what to do with Buster. If he was good in the meantime, Dad might forget, or put it off. And Clint would find a place where he could hide the seal and feed him without Dad or Mom knowing. When school was out for the summer, Clint and Buster would take the *Dolphin* and slip away. They'd sail out of the Canal at night and go to some part of the Sound where people didn't know them; they might go to the San Juans. Some of the islands didn't have any people living on them. Buster and he could have fun there.

But first he had to find Buster.

After chores and breakfast next morning he was free, and he decided to set out on a search. But it wasn't necessary. Buster came home by himself. From the porch Clint saw his round, dark head bob up far out in the channel. Clint ran down to the beach to wait.

The only other thing in sight was a city fisherman, trolling in a boat from one of the resorts. The boat was close enough for Clint to see the man's serious face, his new fishing clothes, and his new-looking gear. Probably he was a new fisherman, too; he was working inshore, where his chances weren't very good; and he was trolling too fast for king salmon, though he might hook onto a silver.

While Clint was making this mental criticism, the fisherman had a strike. His rod arched suddenly, and when the motor stopped the boy could hear the line singing off the reel. Fifty yards astern the salmon flashed up out of the water, walking on his tail—a small silver, quick as dynamite. He failed to shake the plug, and disappeared again. Clint heard the slower sound of the reel as the fisherman put on the drag.

"He'll lose him—but he'll learn," Clint thought. "Now where's Buster?"

Buster wasn't in sight; but after a minute his head popped up a hundred feet from shore, only to disappear again. The line had stopped running out and there was the slow grind of the reel as the fisherman horsed the salmon in.

"Now he will lose it!" Clint thought. He wanted to shout to the fisherman to keep his rod up and let the salmon run—but fishermen don't like advice. A hundred feet astern of the boat the salmon broke water in a desperate leap, and disappeared. The slow grind of the reel stopped, then began again. Clint groaned.

"Don't horse him in; let him run!" He hadn't mean to say it out loud, but his voice shouted what he was thinking.

"Mind your own business!" snapped back over the water.

The salmon was still on, and the line was coming in more easily. Maybe the man would have beginner's luck and drag the fish right up to the boat; but he'd never be able to gaff a silver while it was full of fight.

Suddenly, fifty feet astern of the boat, Buster's head bobbed up, holding the struggling salmon crosswise in his mouth. The sound of the reel stopped while the fisherman stared. The boy could see his amazed white face and his open mouth.

Buster swam toward the boat. The salmon in his mouth made him look as though he were grinning. He was twenty feet from the boat when the fisherman found his voice and shouted:

"Go away, brute! Scat! Go away!"

"It's all right!" Clint shouted. "He won't hurt you!"

Buster sat up, out of water to his shoulders, and looked in surprise from the fisherman to Clint. Then he disappeared with a smooth lunge. Clint saw the line come taut, and slacken as it lost its catch. The fisherman was reeling in his broken line when Buster walloped out on the beach at Clint's feet. He was smiling around the salmon, which he held in his mouth; and his eyes and bobbing head told Clint:

"This is a big day! See what I caught for us! Isn't it fun?"

The fisherman didn't think it was fun.

"Hey, what the heck is going on?"

Clint took the mangled fish from Buster's jaws and held it up by the gills.

"Here's your salmon. Buster was trying to help you!"

The fisherman started his motor with a yank and came charging into shore. His face was red with anger, and it got redder when he failed to stop the motor in time and ran up hard on the beach. He jumped out and stared at Clint and Buster.

"What's going on here? First you try to

tell me how to fish, and then that walrus steals my salmon!"

"He wasn't stealing it," Clint explained. "He's a pet seal and he often helps me fish; I guess he was trying to help you."

"Any time I want help from kids or wild animals, I'll let you know!"

The fisherman took the salmon from Clint and looked at it as if he were going to cry.

"It's ruined."

"Just a few teeth marks," Clint said. "Anyway, you would have lost him. You can't gaff a silver salmon while he's still full of fi—"

"Don't tell me what I can't do!" The angry little man raised his voice and went on scolding. Neither of them noticed Mom coming down from the house until she was standing beside them.

"What happened?" She looked at the mangled fish, and then at Buster, who had fish scales on his whiskers. "Oh, I'm sorry."

The fisherman took off his new fishing hat.

"Forget it, ma'am." He threw the salmon into his boat. "It's just one of those things. Worst part of it was seeing that brute come up on the end of my line—scared me out of ten years' growth."

Clint looked at the little fisherman and began to laugh. It was the last thing he wanted to do, but he couldn't help himself.

The fisherman glared at him.

"What's so funny?"

Mom gave Clint a warning look and spoke soothingly to the fisherman.

"I'm very sorry about this. If there's anything we can do—"

"Forget it!"

He turned abruptly and tried to push his boat into the water. But it had run too hard aground and wouldn't budge.

Clint took hold of the bow. "I'll help you."

"Never mind."

"Let me help, too." Mom took hold of the bow on the other side.

"It isn't necessary." The little man puffed and pushed.

But it was. He made his angry departure with the help of Mom and Clint, while the seal barked encouragement.

"Forget it!" he called again as he drifted away on the outgoing tide, pulling at the starter rope.

Clint would have been glad to forget the whole thing, but he knew Mom wouldn't. The worst part of it was that the fisherman thought Clint was having fun at his expense. Fun! Buster had just added the last straw to his undoing. Clint never felt less like having fun than he did now!

14. THE LOGS

THERE wouldn't have been any expedition that day if Clint had had his wish. But the boys from Big River were already on their way. And Mom was wonderful. She laughed about the little fisherman who had been scared out of ten years' growth, and she went ahead making things for the picnic as if nothing had happened since the plans were made.

Everything was ruined for Clint. But he forgot it while he and Buster waited for the boatful of boys to come in to the landing. There were three Decker boys this time: big Len, and Phil, who had grown a lot since last year, and six-year-old Harry. George Lawson had brought his lively twelve-year-old brother Allen, who was the best shortstop in school.

"Hi, Clint!" Len shut off the old outboard motor. "Buster set any more records?"

"He's not a sissy any more, is he?" Phil asked.

"Can you pet him like a dog?" Little Harry, in bright new overalls, stood up for a better look and Len pushed him down again as the boat came to a stop on the beach.

"Ma went to the city today," he explained; "so I have to run the boat with one hand and baby-sit with the other."

Harry's eyes flashed blue as his overalls.

"You do not! Ma says I'm a big boy now!"

Allen held up a seven-pound silver salmon.

"How's that, Clint? Got him on a hand line the other side of the Flats!"

They all piled out, Len holding his twenty-two in one hand and lifting little Harry by the overalls with the other; and they crowded around Buster.

"He looks like a champion, all right."

"Gee, he's big now!"

"Remember when we tried to teach him to swim?"

"Yeah, and he knocked you flat, getting out of the water!"

"Can I pet him? Can I pet him, please?"

"Sure," Clint said. "Buster, this is Harry. He's my friend. Can you roll over for him?"

Buster rolled over.

"Gee, he's cute!"

"Can he do any other tricks?"

Clint asked, "Do you want Allen's fish?"

Buster nodded, as he always did when you said "fish."

"He knows what you say!"

"You can't have it; it's Allen's." Clint shook his head and showed the seal his empty hands.

Buster gave his silly look and fell over dead for a minute. The boys all laughed; then Clint suddenly remembered the shadow that was over Buster, and it didn't seem funny any more.

He forgot again on the way to the harbor, with Buster swimming on his back alongside, as if he could keep up with the slow old boat while he rested.

"You think you're smart." Len opened the throttle wide.

Buster rolled over and dived. While Len was looking for him astern, the seal's head popped up a hundred feet in front of them.

"You are smart," Len said when they caught up with him, giving the seal a half-friendly grin.

At the harbor they tied up to the float. They could have trolled for salmon, but instead they lay on the sun-warmed planks fishing for pogies that they didn't want and looking down into the underwater world: the silent-moving fish, the seaweed forests waving in the tide, and the hand lines let down from one world into another. It seemed to hypnotize little Harry, who kept inching over the edge of the float, looking down, until someone hauled him back by the overalls. At times Len bawled him out.

"If you fall in the drink, you'll walk back on the beach and stay with Mrs. Barlow."

Mom had wanted Harry to stay at the house with her, but nothing could keep him from going with the big boys once he had been told he could.

The fishing ended when Len started shooting at the pogies with his twenty-two. There was an argument about where the fish really were. Clint said they weren't where they seemed to be because of the refraction of light in water.

"You and your big words!" Len told him. "The pogies are there and I can see them. That's good enough for me."

Clint put a stick into the water and showed Len how it seemed to bend where it entered the water.

But Len said that didn't prove anything.

"If a stick bends when it gets into the water, a bullet does, too. Don't tell me different!"

You couldn't argue with Len. But it didn't matter. Next minute he forgot the argument and decided it was time to eat. After that, he said, they would do something real.

They ate on the float and talked about swimming. But the water was like ice, and Buster did the swimming for them, cruising around the harbor and coming back every little while. He would pop up beside the float and make coaxing faces, trying to tell them the water was fine. When that didn't work, he sat up in the water and begged.

"It's too cold, Buster."

"We're eating now."

"Come around next Fourth of July!"

Buster looked as if he couldn't believe his ears. He made another cruise of the harbor to show them how good it was, then came back and coaxed again. This time Len bent

down and scooped water over Buster's head.
The seal had never been teased before, but
he took it in good part. Instead of going
away he rolled over on his back and edged
closer to the float.

"He likes it," Phil said.

Clint explained, "He thinks it's a game."

Buster thought it was a game that two
could play. Suddenly he began clapping his
nearest flipper against his side, and a
stream of water that looked as if it had
come from a fire pump shot up onto the
float, soaking Len and splashing the others.

The boys scrambled out of range, laughing and kidding Len, who spat salt water
and tried to wring out his clothes.

"I surrender," he told Buster. "I won't
water-fight with you again!"

But Buster had already thought of another
game and was shooting away across the
harbor like a torpedo. By the time Len had
put on a dry jacket, he was zooming back
again. He came toward the float so fast
that Clint didn't see how he could stop in
time. He didn't stop; at the last second he
jumped clear of the water and landed on
the float between Clint and little Harry,
where there was just enough room for him.
The others crowded round.

"Boy, did you see him take off from the water?"

"He's jet-propelled!"

"He could be in a circus!"

Clint explained proudly, "That's what seals do when killer whales are after them. I never saw Buster do it before. He's going good today!"

Buster wriggled in the admiring circle and pranced on his front flippers as if to say that boys are wonderful; the more of them, the better. In another minute he was off again, flickering under the surface and disappearing. They didn't see him again until he popped up far across the harbor where the water was green with the reflection of fir trees on the shore.

Buster had never been so much fun as he was that afternoon, and Clint had never been as proud of him. But he felt hollow and sick when he remembered that his father was going to get rid of Buster. This was the last time the seal and the boys would be together. Suddenly he didn't care what they did.

But Len had got restless and was starting to load things into the boat.

"We've stuck here long enough. We'll

take a look around the harbor and see
what's doing."

They were near the log boom, with Buster streaking ahead of the boat, when Len
had an idea. He slowed the motor and
turned in toward shore.

"Let's have a look at your old man's logs,
Clint."

They coasted by, close to the slender
boom sticks linked with chains, and the ends
of fir logs that floated row on row.

"Your Dad sure has a nice raft!" George
Lawson said.

"I bet he has a million feet!" Allen
guessed.

"Half a million," Clint told him.

Harry stood up to look at the island of
logs.

"I could walk all over there!"

Len sat him down with one hand.

"You could get drowned, too. The first
time I catch you on the logs, you'll walk
back and stay with Clint's ma!"

They tied up to a boom stick in shallow
water and followed the shore, walking on
grounded logs; Len held Harry by the
overalls.

The narrow beach was muddy and
broken; at the dump, skids as big as trees
slanted up to the truck road that had been

bulldozed out of the hillside. The skids were worn almost flat by logs rolling down them, and they bristled with bunches of splinters that looked like scrubbing brushes.

Len poked at the splinters with the muzzle of his gun.

"It shows you the weight logs have to throw around."

"Dad's proud of having got all those logs in the water without anyone getting hurt," Clint said.

"Or killed," Allen said. "Two of my uncles got killed in the woods."

Little Harry looked anxious.

"Are they going to roll any logs down now?"

Len shook his head.

"You'd see a logging truck up there if they were."

Clint told him, "The trucks don't work on Saturday."

"I want to go back where Buster is," Harry said.

There wasn't much to see at the log dump, and they started back to the boat, walking on grounded logs. When they were almost there, Len stopped on a big, lopsided log and put down his twenty-two.

"Here, Phil, you baby-sit for a minute. I'm going to have a look at the boom."

"I don't have to be baby-sat!" Harry shouted. "Don't keep saying it!"

"He's just kidding!" Phil sat beside his little brother, and Clint stood on the other side, watching what was going on.

A few yards away Len stepped on a log that moved a little, and he went on over floating logs toward the outside of the boom, with the Lawson boys following. Most of the logs were close together, so it was only a step between them; but sometimes it was a short jump. The boys all took the jumps as if they had been on booms before, but it was tricky without calked shoes.

Beyond the logs the middle of the harbor was streaked with the ebb tide; and at the end of the boom, near the boat, Buster popped up high out of the water. He looked lonesome, waiting for the boys to come back.

"Watch this!" Len called. "I'm the champion log birler of Jefferson County!" He pranced sideways on a log until the dry brown bark on top rolled slowly out of sight under his feet and dark wet bark came up as the log revolved.

"You and who else?" Allen jumped expertly to the other end of the log, pivoting as he went, and the log rolled a little faster under two pairs of feet.

"I'm the champion log birler of Jefferson County and Mason County!"

George was watching quietly from the big log next to them. Clint hoped he would stop the birling. Instead, George took off his shoes and hopped to the center of the log.

"I'm the champion log birler of Puget Sound!"

The three were on deep water, and if they went overboard one of them was likely to get crushed between the logs, or trapped under them.

"Hey, break it up!" Clint called. "Break it up before somebody gets hurt!"

"Oh, yeah?" Len's face was red with exertion. "Go study your books, Clint!"

"I wish they'd stop," Phil said.

The three on the log were working out some plan. Just when Clint was sure one of them was going overboard, Len jumped to the next log, farther out. George, and then Allen, followed, and they started the second log, which revolved easier than the first. The third was still easier. When they were starting the fourth, Clint went out on the neighboring row of logs. There was something nice about the way the logs moved under foot, as if they were alive. But there wasn't any sense in stirring them up. He stopped near the log the three were birling.

"I wish you'd break it up, fellows. That's too tricky without calks."

"You're talking to champions," Len told him, with his feet flying. "You haven't seen anything until you've seen a two-way roller."

"It's O.K., Clint," George assured him. "We worked this out on the boom at home."

"Wait till you see our two-way roller!" Allen said. "You'll be riding it, too!"

Maybe the boys knew what they were doing, but Clint was sorry it was Saturday, with no boom hands around and no trucks coming to the log dump. He went back to join Phil and Harry on the lopsided log. He watched Buster amuse himself while he waited for the boys. The seal came out from under the boom and rose high out of the water astern of the boat. When he saw that the boys hadn't returned, he rolled over on his back and swam in an easy circle. Next minute he disappeared, and when Clint saw him again he was out in the harbor beyond the boom.

"It's no fun just sitting here," Harry complained. "I want to go back to the boat."

"In a little while," Phil told him. "The two-way is just starting to roll!"

The boys were working back toward

shore on the next row of logs, spinning them in the opposite direction from the first row.

Phil began taking off his shoes.

"I'm going to get in on this. Will you stay with Harry a minute, Clint?"

"I wish you wouldn't, Phil. It looks like a good way to get drowned."

"It's easy! You'll see!"

Phil was off to join the others on the boom.

"ALL ABOARD FOR THE ROLLER!" Len shouted. "HERE GOES!"

He ran out on the first row of rolling logs, hopping from one to the next and giving each one a push with his feet to keep it revolving. At the end of the rollers he ran along a log that hadn't been birled and started back on the logs that were revolving the other way.

George and Allen followed Len out and back on the rolling logs; the second time around Phil followed them. The logs were turning slowly, and it wasn't as dangerous as Clint had thought. Clint knew he could ride the two-way roller, and he would show the others if he weren't minding Harry. When Clint saw Phil coming back, he began taking off his shoes.

"Try it!" Phil urged. "I'll stay with Harry. The roller's going good now!"

It was easier than it looked—if you were used to floating logs; and it was fun. On the third time around Clint got into the spirit of the game. He was as sure-footed as the others, and he went flying out on the offshore roller. Len, Allen and George were just ahead of him, and Phil was taking the jumps beside him. From somewhere behind he heard Harry call.

"Who's watching Harry?" Clint asked.

"Len," Phil told him. "It's Len's turn."

But Len was up ahead. As he turned to start back on the inshore rollers, his eyes swept the boom and he yelled:

"Where's Harry? HARRY!"

It was like a bad dream after that, with everyone running crazily over the boom, looking for Harry. He was gone, except for a pair of little shoes on the lopsided log beside the twenty-two and a name that echoed from the shore.

"HARRY! HARRY!"

The shoes meant that Harry had gone out on the boom. Now he was probably under the logs. Clint saw Phil's tear-stained face as he ran about searching; and he saw Len's desperate look as he let himself down between the ends of the moving logs and disappeared with a lunge.

Harry was down there somewhere. But the only hope of finding him and coming out alive was to go under from open water. While Clint was thinking that and running to the edge of the boom, he was saying inside himself that he hated all logs. In the woods they rolled on loggers and killed them, and in the water they drowned children. Dad had been so careful, and so proud that no one had got hurt. And while he was thinking that everything was safe, the logs were drowning Harry.

At the edge of the boom he let himself into the icy water between the boom stick and the end of a log. Holding on with one hand he looked down for a moment. In the shadow of the boom he could see bottom ten feet below; but a little farther in everything ended in darkness; he would have to feel his way. He took a deep breath.

"Here goes!"

Looking down again, he noticed part of the sand and seaweed blotted out by something sailing through the water. There was a gleam of bright blue. Harry's new overalls! He raised his head and yelled:

"He's here, coming from under the boom!"

He started to dive, but checked himself because Harry's body was coming up rapidly. Under it was a gray, mottled form. He scrambled back on the boom stick in time to grab the overalls as they broke through the surface. Harry seemed to have no weight as Clint started to lift him; then suddenly he was heavy, and Buster's pleased face looked up from the water at Clint's feet.

Clint held Harry upside down to get the water out of him, while bare feet pattered on the logs as the others hurried over.

"Buster brought him out," Clint told them. "Pushed him from underneath, the way seals do with their babies if they fall in before they can swim."

Harry moved his arms. "He's still alive!"

There was no more panic. They got Harry into the boat and covered him with dry jackets. George blew into his mouth, and he and Clint gave Harry artificial respiration while Len drove the boat out of the harbor and toward home, with Buster swimming happily alongside.

Before they reached the landing Harry was breathing for himself; And he was alive enough to whimper as they carried him up to the house.

Dad was home. He and Mom didn't ask any useless questions. Dad called Dr. Jones, while Mom put Harry to bed in the downstairs bedroom. All the boys had been in the water, and Mom sent them upstairs to find dry clothes while she looked after Harry and Dad made coffee.

There wasn't much talking until Dr. Jones came. He felt Harry's pulse, looked under his eyelids, listened to his breathing, and chucked him under the chin.

"He's all right. Just a little shock and immersion. Nothing to worry about now, except pneumonia. He'd better stay here overnight." He listened through his stethoscope again. "Nice and clear. He couldn't have been under long."

"Must have been half an hour," Len said.

"Seemed more like an hour to me," George said. "But I guess it couldn't have been that long."

"It was ten minutes at least," Allen thought.

Clint remembered what he had done, and he tried to fit it into time. Going out on the two-way roller, he had heard Harry call. He had gone to the end and come back, and run over to the edge of the boom and let himself into the water just as Buster was pushing Harry from under the logs. All that could have happened in a minute—but it would take an hour to tell everything he saw and thought and felt in that endless minute.

When the boys were leaving, in borrowed clothes, Dad and Clint went with them to the beach. Before getting into the boat they all hugged the seal. Phil kissed the top of his head, and Len spoke to him.

"Thanks, Buster. I sure thank you!" His face was very red, and when he was in the boat, pulling on the starter rope, he looked as if he were going to cry.

The motor caught and puttered steadily, and the boat swung away from the beach, with all the boys waving and calling, "Thanks!"

Dad stooped and put an arm around the seal. "Thanks, Buster!"

Clint wasn't afraid of anything now.

"You aren't going to get rid of Buster, are you, Dad?"

His father smiled as they started up the beach.

"*I'm not* going to get rid of him, boy."

"I'm going to keep him forever, Dad!"

"How long do seals live?"

"About seventeen years."

"That's a long time, boy."

Dad didn't say anything more. He had said *he* wouldn't get rid of Buster. But it seemed to Clint that there was still a shadow over Buster, and that neither of them could do anything about it.

15. VANISHING BAY

THE blue haze of summer hung over the
water and softened the high, wooded
shore. The breeze was just enough to fill
the *Dolphin's* sails as she ghosted up Vanishing Bay. There was only one other boat
in sight, far off, and Buster had dropped
astern to investigate something on his own.

It was the first day of Clint's long-
promised week of vacation, when his only
tie with home was to build his campfire
where it could be seen from the house, or

when he telephoned to say where he was spending the night.

There were a dozen places he wanted to go, but the decision had been made by the light south wind and the incoming tide. He and Buster were on their way to the Big River country, to see the Deckers and the Lawson boys. The bay still stretched miles ahead of the little sloop, but even in mid-channel the buoyancy of deep water was gone. Looking down, Clint could see crabs running sideways over the rippled sand, and a huge flounder lay motionless on the bottom as he passed.

Buster caught up with the *Dolphin* and swam so close that Clint could pat his head; then he zoomed forward, flickering between the rippled surface of the water and the rippled sand. In a minute he was back again, raising his head high out of the water with a funny, questioning look. He seemed to be asking if Clint knew he was sailing in water less than three feet deep.

"Thanks for telling me, Buster. It'll be like this for another two miles. If we visit too long, all the water will be gone!"

The seal cocked his head at "all gone," as if he couldn't believe it.

"That's right," Clint told him. "It'll be all gone!" He showed his empty hands.

Buster gave a look of alarm and fell over backwards.

Clint laughed. Nobody could be as much fun as Buster on a trip like this.

The bay became shallower and Buster led the way, swimming with his head above water as if to tell Clint that he was practically sailing on heavy dew.

Clint could see the Decker farm: the almost square maple tree at the edge of the shore and the weather-beaten yellow house with the Bing cherry tree at one end. The tree was so tall that you could pick cherries out of the attic window. Beyond the house the orchard was like a green cloud, and above it to the south was the newly painted barn. Behind orchard and barn the timbered foothills rolled up to the mountains. The Big River country was only a dozen miles from home, but it had a different climate because it was pocketed among the hills. Clint trailed his hand in the shallow water, which was warm from having come in over the sun-warmed flats.

Buster came alongside again, with his alert questioning look; Clint thought he was reporting warmer water than they had ever sailed in before.

"You're a good pilot, Buster. Keep reporting. We don't want to get into boiling seas, do we?"

The seal barked his agreement.

"We're almost there, anyway. You'll try to be good, won't you, Buster? We'll only stay a couple of hours, because of the tide. Maybe not that long, because Mr. Decker is strict about making the boys work—" He was interrupted by the clanging of the big locomotive bell that Mrs. Decker used for calling the men home from the fields. "Sounds as though we're just in time for lunch—though it's pretty early."

As the *Dolphin* came in toward the landing, Clint saw Len and Phil waving to him from the narrow strip of beach. Behind them were Mrs. Decker with the twin girls, and the older girl holding little Harry's hand. Mr. Decker, carrying a hoe, was hurrying down the path from the house.

"Wonder who they're waiting for?" Clint said. Then he remembered. "Oh, it's for you, Buster! You're a hero! You saved little Harry! Have you forgotten that?"

Buster looked as if he had never heard of such a thing; but it was nice to arrive in a friendly land where people were lined up on the shore, calling and waving.

The welcome the seal got would have been too much for anyone but Buster, who

liked people—the more, the better. All the
Deckers petted him. Mrs. Decker knelt
down and hugged him; and Madge, the red-
haired oldest girl, took snapshots with a
box camera. It was all right when she was
taking pictures of Buster, and of Buster and
Harry. But then there had to be one of
Clint and Buster, and another of Clint,
Buster, and Harry. Mr. Decker, whose face
was sunburned the color of brick, shook
hands with Clint for a second time; and
Mrs. Decker hugged him for owning the
seal that had saved Harry. The girls looked
as if they were waiting their turn, but Len
came to Clint's rescue.

"For crying out loud, Ma! Do you want
to drive him away? Come on, Clint, we
got things to show you!"

Clint made his escape, with Len and Phil
running interference for him, while Buster
stayed behind to further enjoy a hero's
welcome.

"Boy, are we glad to see you!" Phil said.

"We were going to have to hoe spuds all
day," Len told him. "But as soon as the old
man heard it was you and Buster, he gave
us the rest of the day off."

"I can't stay long," Clint said. "I ought to
get out of the bay on this tide."

"Aw, why do you want to hurry?" Phil

asked. "I called George Lawson when we saw your boat; he and Allen will be right over."

"Wait till you see our new boat!" Len led the way. "It's going to be something!"

The unfinished outboard boat was in the shop beside the barn. Clint admired the oak frames, and the cedar planking which was partly on. The boat looked as if it had been building a long time.

"It was Frank's boat," Phil explained, "but he went into the Army just when he got it well started. He wrote that we could have it."

Frank had been one of the big boys when Clint was starting school, and he had always been nice to the younger boys. Giving the boat to his brothers was just what you'd expect him to do.

They were in the shop when the two Lawsons arrived: George with a twenty-two rifle, and Allen with a fielder's glove.

"We got the day off, too," George announced.

Allen said, "You ought to come around oftener, Clint!"

"We got to plan something," Len said. "We don't want to waste the day."

"How about getting up a game?"

"Naw, we'd have to have the girls in it."

"We could work on the boat," Phil suggested.

"Clint's company; we don't want to work him."

But Clint didn't want to be that kind of company.

"I'd rather work on the boat than anything else. Dad and I are going to build one sometime; I want to learn all I can."

Len considered.

"We have a couple of planks ready to put on, except we have to soak them first, so they'll bend. We can get them started before it's time for chow."

They put the planks to soak in the horse trough and weighted the ends down with rocks. Before they were quite through there was a loud clang on the locomotive bell.

"Five minutes to get to the table," Len explained. Let's put one more rock in the middle, so the planks'll bend while they soak."

There was a second deep clang of the bell as the boys were straggling toward the house, and they broke into a run.

The Deckers' old-fashioned kitchen was as big as the Barlows' living room, and the long table was more than big enough for the eleven people around it. But there was hardly room for all the food: fried chicken

186

and venison and ham, pickles and relishes, potatoes and green peas and corn and string beans, and plates piled high with sliced tomatoes. There were homemade bread and hot biscuits, with butter and raspberry jam. And coffee, milk, and buttermilk to wash it all down. For dessert there were pies and cookies.

At home Mom sometimes told Clint that just because there was a lot of food, he didn't have to try to eat it all. But here the boys kept passing him something every minute, and Mr. and Mrs. Decker kept urging him to have more of this, and more of that. It was the biggest meal he had ever eaten.

After lunch Clint found Buster in the pasture, milking a cow. Mr. Decker was looking on, and he objected when Clint tried to drive Buster away.

"Nothing's too good for him," he told the boy. "If one cow's not enough, we got plenty more."

By the time Clint was ready to be on his way, Vanishing Bay had disappeared, leaving a mile of tide-flats between his boat and blue water. There was no hurry after that.

In the cool of the summer afternoon the boys bent the soaked planks on the boat, drawing them in with clamps and driving them down with wedges until they were snugly in place. They took turns holding a flashlight inside the boat and looking from the outside to make sure that no light showed through the seams. After that Len drilled holes through the new planks into the frames, and supervised the driving of the bronze screws.

At school Len was never any good in science; but at boatbuilding, which was a science, too, he was a master. Clint admired the way he worked.

"I'm going to come over and take lessons from you," he said.

"Aw, it's just common sense. Anything's easy when you can get your teeth into it."

Before the last screw was driven the twins came out to the shop to say that it was time to eat again; and there was another big meal in the Deckers' kitchen.

Afterward the boys put up a tent at the edge of the shore, under the big maple tree. George and Allen had permission to stay overnight, and the tent was the only place where they could all be together. Even Buster was there, listening carefully to the talk about building boats and making voyages, and sometimes looking earnestly at the worn copy of *Pacific Motorboat* the boys were studying.

After Len finally blew out the lanterns, the talk continued until one after another the boys dropped off to sleep. Buster apparently went on dreaming about voyages. Once in the night Clint woke and heard the murmur of the incoming tide; and he heard Buster wallop softly out of the tent and down to the beach for a midnight swim.

The first day of Clint's vacation hadn't been the way he planned it; but he wouldn't have changed anything except the food—there wouldn't have been so much of that. And the good food went along with him. When he and Buster were leaving, Mrs. Decker filled an apple box with half a ham, a pail of eggs, butter, green corn, and fresh-baked bread and stuff. Clint had wanted to live on what he got from the water and beach, and it was embarrassing to have enough food for a crew of six.

By midafternoon they had left Vanishing Bay far astern, and the *Dolphin* was passing Quatsop Point in five hundred feet of water. When Buster swam alongside he no longer looked worried as he had in shallow water. Most of the time he was out ahead, or lingering behind to investigate something on his own, and Clint kept a sharp lookout for other boats; there was always the chance of some sportsman shooting at him because he was a seal.

Most of the boats passed at a distance; but this time, when Clint looked astern, there was a small white cruiser in his wake, about two hundred yards away. The cruiser was coming up fast; and Buster's sleek head showed in the water between the two boats. Clint whistled, and then called:

"Buster! Here, Buster!"

Buster's head disappeared; and Clint didn't see any more of him until he popped up alongside. His wet whiskers sparkled, and his look said, "Aren't we having fun!" He dived suddenly, having more fun.

The white power cruiser was very close now, slowing down. It came abreast of the *Dolphin*, thirty feet away, with a young man in dungarees and yachting cap stepping out on deck. Through the open door of the pilothouse Clint saw a bright-haired young woman at the wheel.

"Hi, there!" the young man called. "Is that your seal that was following you?"

"That's right. He's a pet!"

The young man gave him a friendly, searching look.

"Are you Clint?"

The boy was startled. "That's right."

"I'm Tom Martin. I've heard about you from Professor Wills."

Clint was more surprised. "Do you know him?"

"I'm in the department, and we live next door. I read your paper on geoducks."

Clint blushed. "It wasn't very good."

"It was all right!"

The young woman with bright hair leaned out of the pilothouse to listen.

"Joan, this is Clint," the young man said.

"Hi, Clint!" She gave him a friendly smile. "We know about you and your pet seal." She went back to keeping the cruiser clear of the sloop.

"I suppose you know Prof's in California this quarter," Tom Martin said.

"That's right; at the marine station." His being away had been the only disappointment of the summer.

"When he's back we'd like to come out with him and see you."

"We'd sure like to have you! He knows where we live."

"You aren't going there now, are you?"

"It's the other way. Buster and I are cruising for a week, living off the water and the beach."

"Good for you. That's a real experiment!"

Buster came up alongside, with a snort, and the young woman leaned out of the pilothouse.

"Hi, Buster!"

The seal knew that he was among friends, and he rose half out of the water in greeting.

"He's nice, isn't he?"

"You're a good specimen, Buster," Tom Martin said. He smiled at Clint. "I'm hoping to read your notes on the harbor seal."

"You can, when they're finished."

"We'll bring Prof out when he gets back."

"Don't forget!"

Joan waved from the pilothouse, and the motor rumbled softly as the cruiser drew away.

Clint leaned over the side to pat the seal's head.

"Gee—you're famous, Buster! People even know who I am because of you!" Suddenly he noticed the Deckers' box at his feet, and blushed. "Do you know what I did, Buster? I told the Martins we were living off the water, and all the time I had a box of ham and eggs and stuff where they could see it! I must have been excited!"

Buster snorted and frisked as if it were a good joke.

Clint didn't see it that way.

"That settles it, Buster! We're going to leave the food at old Tim Walsh's. It's time we called on him, anyway."

When they sailed into Triton Cove, blue woodsmoke was rising from the stovepipe of Tim's float-house. The little house was covered with shakes that were silver-gray except for the roof, which was thick with moss, and it floated on cedar logs in water that was green with the reflection of trees.

The float-house had been in the quiet cove as long as Clint could remember. The first time he had been there he was about three, and there was a party for Tim Walsh's ninetieth birthday. On the way there in the boat he had wondered how they were going to get ninety candles on a cake. Dad and Mom had talked as if it were something special to live that long; and Clint thought how lucky he was to have been born in time to see someone that old.

Now Tim was a hundred; and the blue smoke from wood he cut for himself showed that he was up and about. His radio was playing loudly because he was deaf.

Where the water shoaled for the beach Clint pulled up the centerboard and took in the mainsail. With only the jib drawing, the *Dolphin* glided up to the old float-house. Clint put one hand on the front porch, and let go the halliard with the other. The only sound above the noise of the radio was the little squeal of the block as the jib crumpled and came down. That and a pleased snort from Buster, who approved of a house where you could dive off the porch into the water.

Clint was tying up when the door creaked open and old Tim stepped out, light and brisk as a dry leaf.

"Welcome, boy!" he shouted. "I have a clam chowder on the stove! Must have known I was having company. Come in, and have a bite while we talk! Bring your seal in, too, there's nothing he can hurt."

The house was all one room. The kitchen was at the back; on one side of the middle there was a ship's bunk, with a big gray cat sleeping on it; on the other side an eating table, and at the front there were a platform rocker and an armchair beside a window, and the loud radio on a shelf. The walls were hung with fishing gear, oars, guns and tools. Everything was as neat as a man would want it.

Tim ladled wonderful-smelling chowder into the bowls that Clint set on the table. Then he brought the black coffee pot and filled the big white cups.

"Fall to, boy!" he shouted. They drew up chairs. "Hear the radio all right?"

Clint shouted that he could.

"Mostly I don't pay attention to it! Turn it on first thing in the morning and let her rip all day. If you listen close there's some of the worst nonsense—but sometimes I hear music. That's life, boy! You want to know how to live to be a hundred?"

"Yes!"

"Live quietly and don't get in a sweat over things. It's like going through a big room. Rush, and you're soon out of it. Let's have more chowder!"

After more chowder they moved to the chairs by the front window, and Tim went on telling Clint how to live a hundred years.

"Live quietly!" he shouted above the noise of the radio. "You'll live longer, and people will like you better. Never had any patience with people who made a big noise! I've seen them come and go. The bigger noise they made the quieter they went away. There were the Hargroves who built a mansion over yonder in 'ninety-one.

Servants and horses and carriages, though there were hardly any roads; and a big sailing cutter; and a steam launch. They blew bugles when they were going to eat. Where are the Hargroves now, boy?"

Clint had never heard of them.

"That was when the railroad was coming through here! Union, where the store is, was going to be another New York. They had a city laid our clear back to the mountains. That was before your time, boy! When the panic of 'ninety-three hit the railroad, people went home. I never heard another sound from the big house across the water. Except one night somebody played 'Taps' on a bugle. Next day they were all gone. . . ."

The boy listened to hear more. But Tim was asleep in the platform rocker, with the gray cat asleep in his lap. Clint turned the radio down. The *Dolphin* was bumping lightly against the porch, reminding him it was time to go; and thick gold sunlight slanted into the room through the back window. When Tim woke, Clint would say good-by to him.

The shaft of gold sunlight made the air seem thick, like seawater full of drifting plankton. It was like being in a cave under the ocean, with Tim, as old as Davy Jones,

196

sleeping in his chair, and the seal and the boy sitting on the cave floor. The thick gold light touched Buster's chest and lit up his whiskered face as if he were smiling. The radio was playing "The Dance of the Hours," and he swayed in time to the music.

When the light reached the platform rocker it began fading as the sun dropped behind the mountains, and the music ended. Old Tim was still asleep.

Clint got up.

"Time to go, Buster."

Outside he noticed the Deckers' box of food still in the sloop. He lugged it into the house and left it on the table without waking the old man.

"We're on our own now," he told the seal as he was casting off. "If we can't catch what we need we'll eat procupine tracks! Want to ride for a change?"

Buster slithered happily into the boat; and as they tacked out of the cove he swayed his head as if he still heard "The Dance of the Hours."

16. END OF SUMMER

THE *Dolphin* sailed close-hauled past Toandos, into the sunset; Clint and Buster were going to spend the last night of their outing at Pirate Bay. Buster, who didn't know where they were going, swam a hundred yards ahead of the sloop, looking back to see which way Clint would turn when he passed Oak Head.

The only boat in sight was a big mahogany cruiser tearing up from the southwest, its bow throwing sheets of spray. Probably some big wheel dashing back to Seattle—one of those people Old Tim said were always in a hurry. If the cruiser held its course, it would pass half a mile to the south, and it would be out of the Canal by the time Clint and Buster made their camp for the night.

The wind was steady and the water swished smoothly past the *Dolphin's* hull as she swept through it. Not like the slashing attack of the cruiser . . . Clint raised his eyes for another look, and was surprised to see the cruiser only a few hundred yards away, foaming toward the *Dolphin*. Now it was almost abreast of Buster's head, which was silhouetted darkly against the sunset water. Clint hadn't expected them to pass so close. . . .

"*Look out!*" A rifle barrel was pointing out of a window on the bridge deck of the cruiser.

Clint grabbed up his twenty-two, aimed between the cruiser and Buster's sleek head, and pulled the trigger.

Crack!

The bullet hit the water a few yards from Buster and skipped past the cruiser's stern.

The seal's head disappeared, and at the same moment there was the crash of a high-power rifle on the cruiser.

Clint held the tiller with his elbow as he reloaded. He didn't think they had got Buster—but just let them try again!

The cruiser came foaming down, a hundred feet away. People stepped out on deck, and a red-haired yachtsman with a rifle shook his fist at Clint.

"You fool!"

"You fool!"

The yachtsman and the boy shouted the words at the same time.

The cruiser rushed by and Clint headed up into her wake. The heavy swells knocked the wind out of the sails and threw everything around. The yachtsman didn't have the good sense to pass a small boat at a safe speed and distance. He probably thought that Clint had tried to shoot the seal, too, and spoiled his chance.

"The fool!"

He was relieved when Buster came up alongside, unhurt, with a squid in his mouth. But as the sloop jogged toward Pirate Bay his thoughts went back to the yachtsman on the mahogany cruiser. There were too many people who thought they had to kill every wild thing they saw. Buster could get shot any time he showed his head out of water.

Clint didn't feel at ease until they were

camped at Pirate Bay and he was broiling a piece of salmon over the coals of their fire. He had caught the salmon trolling off Vineland, and the seal had eaten his share raw. While Clint waited for his own to cook, he talked to Buster.

"I was right here," he said, "lying on the sand, when I heard you sounding off. At first I thought you were a lamb, though sometimes you sounded like someone blowing a little tin horn. You were mad because your mother didn't come. When I showed up, you thought I was your mother."

Urrgh! Urrgh!

"You're a big boy now," Clint continued. "You go on expeditions and catch salmon and get into scrapes. And you swim all the way home from up near Alaska! Why didn't you stay there and be a wild seal?"

Buster hitched forward, rested his chin on the boy's knee, and looked up into his face.

Clint didn't ask him again.

The afterglow was fading behind the Olympics on the other shore by the time the salmon was done.

Clint ate with his fingers, breaking off tender pink pieces and giving an occasional one to Buster.

"You're not supposed to have cooked food, you know."

Urrgh!

When they had finished eating Clint lay by the fire, with his head on Buster's springy back. He crossed his knees, lifting one bare foot against the western sky, and wiggled his toes.

"This is the life!"

He didn't know how much of a life it was for Buster; the seal never moved when he was being used for a pillow.

In the deepening dusk a star came out directly overhead; then another. He heard the wash of the incoming tide, and in the woods above him an owl hooted. Soon he could make out the constellations: Orion, and the Big Dipper, and the Pleiades like a school of candlefish in the sky. He sat up and saw the stars reflected in the water. Miles away, against the dark land, there was an oblong of yellow light—the porch of his home! He piled more wood on the fire so Mom and Dad would be sure to see it.

"Time to hit the sack," he told Buster when the flames began to die down again.

The seal already had his warm sack on. Clint crawled into his sleeping bag and pulled up the zipper.

"Good night, Buster."

Buster wriggled closer to the sleeping

bag, laid his head on the sand, and was asleep—or pretended to be.

The boy watched the stars awhile, then turned over. Next thing he knew Buster was nudging him to get up. He rubbed his eyes and looked around.

In the white morning mist at the edge of the water two great blue herons, like tall shadows, were squawking noisily, as if they were arguing which way to take off.

Buster looked at Clint, his eyes seeming to say, "The silly things are on our beach. Let's give them a good scare!"

Clint shook his head.

"*Sh-h-h!*"

Arguing loudly, the herons took off, with a great flapping of wings and waving of long legs.

Buster was free to talk now and he whined coaxingly and sidled toward the water.

"All right, fellow," Clint told him. "But first I'll get a fire going. I'll need to warm up when we come out!"

After the first shock the water was fine. Clint started to race Buster to the *Dolphin*, which seemed a long way out now that the tide was in. She must be in about ten feet of water. He was only halfway there when he met Buster coming back. So he returned to water of his own depth, and swam down to bottom. It was thick with oysters down there, all busily feeding with their shells open a little and their mantles fluttering. The plankton on which they fed looked like dust drifting in the tide. But it was a mighty dust that fascinated Clint because it provided food for everything in the ocean.

He surfaced for air, then went down again. This time Buster came with him to watch the oysters. The seal always seemed specially pleased when they met under water; at such times he seemed to think that someday Clint would really learn to swim.

It wasn't going to be this time, though. Clint left the water, shivering, and sprinted toward the fire.

After he was warm and dry he felt the glow of the undersea exploration, and as he went about preparing his breakfast salmon he talked to Buster.

"Know what I'm going to do, Buster? I'm going to save my money and buy an Aqualung. That's a new gadget that lets you carry your own air supply under water. With one of those things I'll be able to stay deep down for hours. I'll be a match for you then, Buster! What do you say?"

Buster finished a piece of raw salmon and seemed to think it was a wonderful idea.

"I'll look kinda queer, with the gadget strapped over my face and the tubes going round to the air tanks on my back. But you won't mind that, will you?"

Urrgh! Urrgh!

"Sure you won't!" Clint tossed him another piece of salmon.

"This is the shore of the world, Buster," Clint told him. "There's seven times as much ocean as there is land. That's a lot of water to explore. We're only just beginning." He remembered immediate things, and added: "But it's the last day of this expedition. We want to take something home. We'll begin by trolling for a salmon; and when the tide is lower, we'll dig a mess of clams."

At sunset the *Dolphin* glided in toward Barlow's Landing, with Buster swimming close alongside. Dad and Mom were waiting on the beach, where the dogs barked a welcome; and Jerry waded out to meet the returned wanderers. Clint hadn't expected such a reception. It made him feel as if he were coming home from a voyage around the world.

He dropped the sails as the sloop grounded, and he jumped out, barefoot, to help Dad haul her up on the beach. There was a welcoming uproar, with Dad shaking hands with Clint; Mom hugging him, and Buster adding his barking to the noise of the dogs as they danced around the humans and the seal.

Mom told Clint, "I never saw you looking so brown and thin!"

"And healthy," Dad put in. He and Clint unloaded the camping gear, the sack of butter clams, and the big king salmon Clint had caught a mile from home, when he had almost given up hope of a strike.

As they all moved up the beach toward the house, the boy felt as if he had been away for a long time, and it was good to be home.

"How has everything been?" he asked. "I bet you found it less work without Buster and me!"

Mom told him, "We managed—but we missed you."

"What's happened while I was away?" It seemed as if there had been time for the whole world to change.

"Our logs are gone from the harbor,"

Dad told him. "I got a good price for them. Your mother's ordered a freezer, and I'm going to buy a new hat. I expect there'll be something for you."

"What Clint needs right now is food," Mom decided. "I never saw him so thin. It's a good thing I have dinner ready!"

In the house everything looked strange and familiar at the same time. Clint was too excited, telling about his adventures, to sit down until Mom had served dinner.

He had forgotten about such things as mail; but there was an opened letter at his place at the table.

"Professor Wills wrote to us," Mom explained. "It's for you, too."

The first part of the letter was about the Willses' summer in California, and their plans for returning to Seattle. Then:

As I remember, Clint begins high school this fall. I don't know your plans for him, but he has made a good start in a great new field, and a good science teacher can be a great help to him.

If you decide to send Clint to high school in Seattle, Mrs. Wills and I would be happy to have him stay with us. I'm sure he would find us easy to get along with, and my library would be helpful.

The Proctors next door have four boys and girls of high-school age, all much interested in sailing and fishing. Clint would find them good company.

The Martins, who live on the other side of us, have a small cruiser . . .

Clint looked up from the letter to explain excitedly, "I met the Martins on the way to Triton Cove. They knew who I was because of Buster. They're the swellest people!"

He was still in a glow when he finished the letter. "Gee, that's wonderful!"

"I think it is!" Mom said.

Dad nodded his agreement. "And what's more, with the logs sold we can manage it."

"Gee!" Clint said again.

The window rattled; and he turned to see Buster's funny, eager face, and a flipper knocking against the glass. It was half dark outside, and the seal seemed to be looking through water, reminding Clint not to forget him.

"What about Buster?"

"You can't let a seal stand in the way of your education!" Mom's voice was sharp; but Dad smiled as he spoke.

"You'll be starting school in a few days. Wherever you are, Buster will have to be penned up for most of the next nine months."

Clint hadn't let himself face that.

"I could stay out of school for a year; I'd learn a lot—"

"No!" Mom's voice was like the closing of a door.

Dad answered with a slow smile. "You'd have the same problem to meet next year."

"If I went to high school at Crossroads, I could keep an eye on Buster—"

"It would still mean keeping him locked up so he couldn't do what he wanted to."

It was no use. "I don't feel right about having Buster penned up. I let you send him away—"

"I know," Dad said, "and it didn't work. I hadn't counted on his being so fond of people."

"That's it. He loves people, and he's smart and full of fun."

Dad nodded. "No matter where he was turned loose, he'd come back here, or get shot on the way—"

"What can we do?"

Dad spoke quietly, "Frank Ives stopped by while you were away. He'd heard about Buster—"

Mr. Ives had a big fishing boat with special equipment, and he collected live specimens for aquariums and zoos.

Dad went on, "Frank said he'd be glad to

take Buster and find a good home for him—"

"In a zoo?" Clint was shocked.

"Why not? Buster likes people—but most of them would try to kill him if he were free in the Sound. The same people would be nice to him if he were in an aquarium. He would be safe there, and he'd see the best side of people."

Mom said, "It's the only place for him."

"I won't give him up!" While Clint was saying that he remembered the mahogany cruiser tearing out of the sunset, and the redheaded sportsman with the rifle. There were hundreds like him; and any moment of freedom Buster had might be ended by a bullet.

Clint took a deep breath, as if he were going under water.

"Mr. Ives can take Buster, Dad."

A smile shone on his mother's face. "Clint, you're growing up! You'll be a credit to us."

Dad said, "It's the right decision."

Clint steadied his voice. "We won't take any money for him."

"No, boy."

"And Mr. Ives will have to find the best kind of a place for him."

"I'll see to it."

"And, Dad—"

"Yes?"

"I don't want to know where they take him."

His father nodded.

Buster had disappeared from the window; and Clint looked soberly at Professor Wills's letter. It was like a new world opening before him; he felt strange and alone because the world on which he had opened his eyes that morning had ended with stunning suddenness.

17. THE LITTLE SEA

A FEW months before, Clint might have
taken to the woods at the thought of
going out to dinner with Aunt Harriet. It
didn't exactly thrill him now. Still he had to
hand it to her for getting him to high
school in Seattle. It was worth it just to see
the Oceanographic Laboratory where he
was visiting now with Professor Wills.

It was after hours; but there was no real
"after hours" in the laboratory, with sea
water circulating day and night in tanks

where things lived and grew and changed. It was a magic place where you could see things that were happening in the deep ocean. You could also look through glass into the future. One tank had a piece of the great electric cable that was going to be laid across Puget Sound. The cable wasn't finished yet, but in the tank you could see it in salt water with barnacles growing on it. That was so the engineers could decide on the best protection for its steel shell. When Clint looked at it long enough, he forgot that he wasn't under water.

To Clint the most fascinating place of all was the machine shop downstairs, where equipment for exploring the sea was made and repaired. On a platform at one end of the shop there was a model of Puget Sound showing all the channels and headlands and islands. There were gears that represented the sun and moon. You could set them to make any tide you wanted to study; while salt water circulated through the channels, fresh water ran in from rivers that came down from the mountains. The model was about twenty feet long, and a cycle of the tide took minutes instead of hours.

Professor Wills looked at his watch.

"We should have time to run through a

tide before your aunt calls for you. Is there any special tide you would like this time?"

Clint said, "I'd like to see the way it was this morning."

"Nothing easier!" The professor consulted a tide table, set the sun and moon, and turned a switch.

Smoothly the tide moved in through Admiralty Inlet, dividing at Foulweather Bluff, with part of it swelling into Hood Canal and the rest going on through the main channel of Puget Sound.

At other times Clint had tried to watch all the inlets at once; but this time he followed the tide into Hood Canal, and south along Toandos. At the end of the peninsula it turned southwest, and at Oak Head it divided again, part of it continuing southwest, and part of it moving past Pirate Bay, into the inlets to the north.

As Clint watched, the model seemed to grow in size until it was like watching the tide moving through the real inlets. He could almost see the Deckers' weather-beaten house reflected in the water as it covered the flats of Vanishing Bay. Farther south it was rising over the beach at Barlow's Landing, and still farther south it flowed into Pleasant Harbor and Triton Cove. By raising his eyes a little he could see it moving through all the waterways of Puget Sound, pushing through narrows and sweeping around islands until the tide stood still in all the brimming channels. It was ebbing when Professor Wills spoke.

"It sounds as if your aunt is here for you."

Clint had been so absorbed in watching the ebb tide circulate around islands in the opposite direction from the flood that he hadn't heard anything. Now he heard the tooting of a familiar horn.

"That's her," he said. "I wish she'd waited until the tide was out."

"We can make plenty more tides." Professor Wills turned off the machinery.

On the way out he said, "Clint, could I get you to read your paper on the harbor seal at a meeting we're having next week?"

He wondered if he had heard right. "You mean to your students?"

The professor's eyes twinkled behind his glasses. "There may be some faculty members present."

"But I'm only in high school!"

"It is a good paper, and you know a lot about seals. That's more important than how old you are."

Clint had a terrifying picture of himself reading his paper to a roomful of college students and professors. Maybe he'd forget to wear his shoes or a necktie, and everyone would laugh. Anyway, they'd wonder why a boy was there, telling them things they knew better than he did.

"Gee, it's nice of you to ask me, but I don't know—I don't see how I could do it—"

He must have looked upset, because Professor Wills didn't insist. "I know you would make a good job of it—but think it over. You can let me know tomorrow."

"I will," Clint told him, "and thank you for asking me."

When he got into the car he was still a little dazed. Aunt Harriet had to ask him twice where he would like to eat.

"All the places you have taken me have been swell."

"Would you like the Salmon Bay Terminal?"

"That would be great, Aunt Harriet!" It was his favorite place.

She started the motor, and turned west. "I have good reports about your work in school, Clint."

"Things are easy when you're interested in them. I can see why you wanted me to go to high school here. I sure thank you." He thought he should tell her about Professor Wills asking him to read his paper at a meeting—but he couldn't quite believe it himself. And he didn't want to do it.

The restaurant was on a dock on the ship canal through the city and its glass front looked out on piers where the Alaska fishing fleet tied up for the winter. Halibut schooners, purse seiners, gill netters and trollers were crowded in as close as cars in a downtown parking lot, and their masts and poles made a thick forest. Among the boats Clint saw Captain Johanson's sturdy old *Snow Queen*. There were other boats Clint had seen at different times; and he was so busy looking that he kept forgetting to eat. It wasn't polite to Aunt Harriet, and he tried to make up for it by telling her the news about his paper on the harbor seal. When he told her, it seemed real for the first time, but as alarming as ever.

His aunt wasn't as surprised as he expected her to be, but she looked very pleased.

"That's good, Clint! Did you tell Professor Wills you'd do it?"

"I said I'd think it over—I don't see how I can do it. There'll be students and professors who know so much more than I do—"

"Not about seals," Aunt Harriet insisted.

"None of them will have your first-hand experience. And Professor Wills wouldn't have asked you if he hadn't thought you had something real to give."

"I guess you're right," Clint admitted.

"You'll do it, then."

Clint didn't think so. He was looking through the glass wall of the restaurant, out to the pier where Captain Johanson's old halibut schooner was packed among other boats. He could see the nested yellow dories, and the deck where he had once said good-by to Buster. Suddenly he knew why he didn't want to read his paper at the meeting.

"Why not?" Aunt Harriet wanted to know.

"It's because of Buster," he told her. "It's really his paper; he did all the things I wrote about. Now I don't even know where he is—and I don't want to talk about him."

His aunt looked at him strangely.

"But, Clint, you said you didn't want to know where Mr. Ives took him!"

"I know. But it didn't work. I don't feel right about him." When he had admitted it, he knew how bad he felt.

Aunt Harriet opened her handbag and rummaged in it.

"You want to know, then?"

She took out a newspaper clipping and unfolded it.

"I have had this for two weeks, wondering if I ought to show it to you."

Clint looked eagerly at the newspaper picture of a harbor seal and a group of children. The children were standing at the edge of a pool, admiring the seal that was sitting up in the water as straight as a penguin. His nose was in the air and on his face there was a wonderful, silly look that told you he was getting ready to fall over backwards in pretended disappointment. The clipping was from an Oregon newspaper.

New Seal Star Attraction at Ocean Beach Aquarium

Buster, the harbor seal at Ocean Beach, is winning more friends than all the other animals in the Aquarium. His good humor and love of fun have made him a favorite with adults, including his keeper, Norton Smith, who declares Buster is the smartest seal and best comedian he has ever known. As for the children, the accompanying picture gives some idea of what they think of Buster. His reputation is enhanced by the fact that recently, in his native Puget Sound, he saved a child from drowning. But it is Buster's many tricks that endear him . . .

Clint finished reading the story with a new, happy feeling.

"I'm glad you showed it to me, Aunt Harriet. I'm glad Buster's having fun."

"That's the way I feel," Aunt Harriet said.

"I should have known Buster would come through," Clint told her. "He likes people, the more the better."

His aunt smiled at him proudly.

"That would complete your paper, wouldn't it, Clint? . . . If you ever felt that you wanted to do anything about it—"

"I *am* going to do something about it! I'm going to read the paper for Professor Wills!"